Million Dollar Heartache

T. Renee

BookLocker
Saint Petersburg, Florida

ISBN 978-1-64719-294-5

Published by BookLocker.com, Inc., St. Petersburg, Florida.

The characters and events in this book are fictitious. Any similarity to real persons, living or dead, is coincidental and not intended by the author.

Library of Congress Cataloguing in Publication Data
Renee, Tiffany
Million Dollar Heartache by T. Renee
Library of Congress Control Number: 2021900029

Printed on acid-free paper.

Booklocker.com, Inc.
2021

DEDICATION

To you,

To the women who don't want to be rescued—the ones that just want to be respected and loved. To you—my classic ladies who still enjoy a little modesty and mystery. To my loyal lovers, men and women alike—to those that know that real love is worth every heartache—that it's worthy of every and any sacrifice.

I love you my darling divas,
Nicole, Blythe, Ain and Arica.
Cheers to you!
Never settle, love hard and smile often.

And to my mother, the woman who taught me to love a good tearjerker, and to find the joy in the saddest of moments. I love you always, forever, to the moon and back.

All my love.
Always,
T. Renee

INTRODUCTION

Thursday morning, just two days until Christmas and New York City was all aglow. There were lights, ornaments, and icicles everywhere. Decorations hung from mailboxes, public and private buildings, and nearly every street pole on every block around the city. Of all the things New York did well, they did Christmas best of all.

The brisk December air was much more inviting outside than the cold dark stillness that lay inside the apartment that had once belonged to the Wade family. In the pre-war apartment building on the two-hundred block of West 74th Street, Oceana Veritas Wade stood near the window that offered the best view of the city in the apartment that she'd grown up in, an apartment that now belonged to the bank.

The nearly bare apartment where she spent her entire adolescent life would soon be occupied by a complete stranger and she couldn't have cared less. After her father died when she was twelve, the apartment felt less like a home and more like a cage and Oceana felt a lot like a bird with clipped wings desperate to take flight. But with her mother as her jury and jailer, compassionate release was out of the question; kindness and compassion exited the apartment immediately upon her father's death. It had been twenty years since her father passed but she mourned him as if it were yesterday, her heart hurt for him in a way it couldn't for her mother who had died just nine days earlier. But when it came to Oceana's mother, sorrow was just a fleeting thought.

Oceana's mother, Maritza Giselle Wade was a woman of low and loose morals with little to no compassion for anyone aside from herself and that included her own daughter. Maritza earned her millions by way of deceit and treachery which was the same way her own mother had earned hers. They both lied, stole, and even feigned injury to hustle people out of their money; all deplorable actions but they were nothing compared to their coup de gras which was that each woman had married a wealthy man late in his life, bore him one child and inherited his entire fortune and then squandered it solely on themselves.

Oceana's father was a pretty wealthy man. He had earned his millions in architecture. He traveled the globe for years designing grand structures and exquisite statues. It wasn't until the latter part of his life that he began to yearn for some stability and a family. Maritza was a beautiful, seductive woman with a keen sense of timing and she swooped right in and sold herself as the very thing Lloyd Wade was looking for…and he bought her.

Neither Maritza or her mother had children because of some innate female yearning. Both women hated children, which is why they both only had one, and they only had that one child because it was a good business move. When it came to their finances the two women left nothing to chance. When a signature was illegible or lacking, the bond of blood could never be denied.

Lloyd Wade loved Oceana from the moment she took her first breath, she was the greatest love of his life. While Maritza shopped, traveled and partied, Lloyd stayed at home and doted on Oceana until his very last breath, it would have broken the man's heart to know that his darling daughter had been left to financial ruin by the pretender of a wife he'd left his fortune to. It had taken Maritza no time at all to squander away everything it took Lloyd a lifetime to earn, and not only did she spend everything he had saved but she also spent a great deal of what he never had.

Since Lloyds death, Maritza had blown through all of the sixty-three million he'd left behind for her and Oceana to live on. In addition to spending all of his money, she also stopped paying the taxes on the apartment he'd been so very fond of and had invested a great deal of time and money to restore.

Now deceased, Maritza had managed to leave behind thirteen million dollars of debt to the daughter she almost loved. The apartment had been seized by the state. The artwork it had taken Oceana's father a lifetime to collect was stripped from the walls and put up for auction along with anything and everything that would fetch a decent price.

It was barely ten o'clock that Thursday morning when Oceana left her post in front of the window and slowly walked past the few scattered boxes that lay on floor of what used to be her living room. It had been over a decade since she'd last stepped foot in that apartment. Her fondest childhood memories were the ones of her and her father at home alone in the apartment listening to music, watching the ballet on television, him reading to her, her singing to him; moments in time filled with love, all his life's work that once filled each room was now gone. A decade's worth of memories, a lifetime worth of hard work was boxed up and emptied out in less than a week.

A guitar chord pierced though the silence and commanded Oceana's attention. She quickly pulled her cellphone from her pocket and silenced the blues melody, after a brief moment of indecision about wanting to speak with the heartless soul sucking *SOB* who had so quickly taken the only evidence she had that someone had loved her, she glanced down at the phone in disgust and decided to take the call and get it over with.

"Hello?"

"Hello. Oceana?"

"Yes, this is she."

"Hi, this is—"

Annoyed by the caller before he had even begun to speak, Oceana decided to help him get to the point. "Yes, yes I know who it is. Matt Cartridge from Bowman Law, *yes*, I know. So, you've taken all my father's stuff to pay my mother's debt and now you're calling to tell me what? There's more? She still owes more?"

Matt cleared his throat and exhaled loudly. "No. No, there's no more. Your father had a great deal of fine things, a lot of them with pretty high pre-appraised value, more than enough to pay off your mother's debt. I was calling because there's a small amount left over that I thought you'd like to have before the holiday. I'm really sorry things turned out the way that they did. From what I've heard, you and your father were really close. Must be tough on you to see all his things gone."

A sigh of relief that came from deep inside Oceana echoed in the phone. After twenty years no one had truly expressed any real condolence towards her for the loss of her father. It wasn't the money that relieved her, it was the remorse, it was Matt's empathy an actual acknowledgement of her pain.

"Yeah, we were close. It was hard to watch his—never mind. What's done is done. But thank you for respecting his things the way you did and not just tossing them around. That meant a lot to me and I just wanted you to know I appreciate it."

"No problem at all Ms. Wade. Well, I'll be in the office today until about noon, I've got a cashier's check here for you twenty-three thousand dollars, it's yours whenever you're ready to come get it."

"I'm ready. God, I'm beyond ready to get out of this place. I'll see you soon Mr. Cartridge."

PART ONE

SERENDIPITY

CHAPTER ONE

"Oceana."

Gregory Edwards continued to scroll through an online file he'd been reading as he waited for Oceana's response. After five minutes of waiting and still no reply he shoved the keyboard in front of him and mashed the intercom button on his phone again.

"Oceana!"

"Yes, Mr. Edwards?"

"Come see me in my office."

"Be right there, Sir."

Greg leaned back in his high-back leather chair and exhaled in frustration and waited for Oceana to come and speak with him.

Two minutes after she'd been summoned, Oceana entered Greg's office carrying a legal pad and pen ready to take instruction.

Greg shook his head and gave a quick huff. He whole heartedly disapproved of having Oceana as his assistant but he'd run off nine temps before her in less than five months and the agency the firm worked with let him know Oceana would be the last they sent for him, so he tolerated her out of pure necessity. She annoyed him but she wasn't incompetent.

Oceana looked at Greg and smiled before taking her seat. She was very well aware of his dislike for her but she didn't much care because she didn't like him either. She disliked lawyers in general, she hadn't met any honest ones in the course of her lifetime but the fact that Greg disliked her without any *good* reason made her dislike him even more. He always had something negative to say to her; *her penmanship was too swirly, her clothes were too shabby, she cared too much, was way too emotional about his clients*, it was always something. Working for an attorney's office was far from her idea of a dream job but it was a job that paid well so she tolerated him.

"You wanted to see me?"

"Yes, Oceana, clearly. I told you to put together an expense report for the month every month and I don't see this month's report. Where is it?"

"You mean for October?"

"Yes. October."

"But it's not the end of the month yet."

"That's not what I asked you."

"But I do the monthly report at the end of the month every month and it's only the 26th, so I haven't done October's yet."

"I need the report now."

Oceana took a breath and smiled as she got up from her seat. "I'll start working on it as soon as I get back from lunch."

Baffled by her reply Greg jerked forward in his chair and swiftly shook his head. "Are you hearing impaired? I said, *now*."

Once she was halfway out the door again, Oceana took another long breath. She stood silently for a moment with her eyes closed and her hand on the doorknob, and then she turned and looked at Greg and smiled. "I heard you Mr. Edwards however, I have plans for lunch that I can't break but I promise I will get the expense report done as soon as I come back. If it's something you need done right this second, I'd be more than happy to bring you my files and you can start putting the report together yourself."

Disgusted by the assumption that he would be willing to do *her* work Greg leaned forward over his desk and opened his arms wide and flipped his palms up in aggravation. "Your files? You want to bring me your files to do *your* job? You're kidding, right? You do understand how this works, right? I'm *your* boss, I pay you. You report to me. You do what *I* say."

"I'm very well aware of my position Mr. Edwards. Yes, I know how this works. I also know that your expectation for me to have a month end report done *before* the end of the month *without* having been asked to do it before hand is unreasonable. I also know that as far as temps go, there's none in the building that I can go and ask a favor of for *you* which just leaves me... me and you. And *I* have plans for my lunch hour which just leaves *you*. Also, I know I report to you which is why I came to you a month ago and asked you if it would be okay if I pushed my lunch back to one o'clock for today to which you said, *fine* and to *put it on the calendar* which I did... a month ago. I'm not an unintelligent person Mr. Edwards, I know you're my boss and I know I report to you and I know my job is to do what you ask me to do— within reason, I don't see this request as reasonable."

Greg sat dumbstruck, with his mouth hanging open and glared as he watched Oceana slip out the door and close it behind her. He wanted to storm after her and fire her, he wanted to give the self-righteous little hippie a piece of his mind but he didn't, instead he threw his pen across his desk and huffed and puffed until he calmed himself down. The family friendly, employee friendly firm where he worked did not tolerate public berating. Greg disliked his firm almost as much as he disliked Oceana but it was the one reputable firm that was willing to take a chance on a guy like him; an arrogant, good looking guy from the wrong side of the tracks of Chicago. The managing partners of the firm disliked Greg as much as he disliked them but their largest account was his closest friend in life so when he applied for a position with their office, they begrudgingly gave it to him, and in so the dance of disdain between him and them ensued. Greg had the least desirable office in the building which was three stories high and ascended in level of importance and expertise.

Despite his having not lost a case since he started over five years ago, Greg's office was on the ground floor at the end of the hall not too far away from the public restrooms. The partners all treated him like shit it was only fitting that he should have to walk down the hallway and smell it too. Despite his office location and the smell that you had to sometimes walk through to get to him, Greg was in high demand, the most requested attorney in the firm despite the lack of referrals from his colleagues, and in spite of how he was treated, he never let it bother him too much. Instead of getting mad and stewing over any situation, he decided he'd just be better than everyone else there. He might have to smell shit everyday but they were the ones always appearing to be in need of an Alka-Seltzer sandwich each time he shook the hand of a new client and smiled and winked in their direction. Today, he decided to give Ocean a small dose of *screw you*.

Greg smiled to himself as he reached for the intercom button on his phone. "Oceana?"

"Yes, Mr. Edwards?"

"Oh, good you're still here." Greg knew Ocean needed to be his assistant as much as he needed to have an assistant, she was always filling in on weekends for other temps trying to make a little extra cash and while secretarial work was something Greg despised doing, he decided today it wasn't all that bad especially not if doing it helped him prove a point. "I'm waiting on your files so I can get started on the expense report, and Oceana…"

"Yes, Mr. Edwards?"

"After you're done with lunch you can head home for the day, I won't be needing you for anything else. Please clock out when you leave."

CHAPTER TWO

Since she relocated to Seattle nine months ago Oceana had yet to completely unpack the few boxes she'd brought with her from New York. Her quaint one bedroom was a shoebox compared to the breathtaking Upper West Side apartment she'd grown up in, but she liked it where she was now much better.

While she hadn't completely unpacked, she had completely settled in to her new place, her new life and her new-found happiness; but there was still one lurking item that encroached on her new-found sense of happy, and that Saturday morning that nuisance decided to wake her up at eight o'clock.

"Hello?"

"Good Morning Ms. Wade, this is Fritz with Sampson's Crematorium, I hope I'm not disturbing you?"

"Oh no Fritz, I was just sleeping is all but I'm up *now* at eight o'clock in the morning on a Saturday." Oceana sighed and curled up on her side and shut her eyes. There was a momentary silence on the line but Ocean knew he hadn't hung up... he never hung up.

"Ms. Wade, I was calling again to discuss the matter of your mother."

Oceana chuckled and sighed. "Well, she's still dead isn't she, Fritz?"

"Ma'am?"

Oceana rolled over onto her back and sighed again. "Don't be so serious Fritz, it's not like she can hear me, and even if she could there's not much she could do about it."

"Ms. Wade, can you please be serious for just a moment?"

Ocean sat up in her bed and fluffed the comforter around her. "Okay you want me to be serious—well, I *seriously* don't care what you do with my mother's ashes—toss 'em, dump 'em off a cliff, I really don't care. Just stop calling me about them."

Ocean quickly hung up after the last word had fallen from her mouth, intentionally preventing the frustrated but well-meaning crematorium owner from trying to rebuke anything she had said. After sliding her cell phone back on the night stand, she fell back down on the bed and groaned in frustration. "Even in death you still find a way to torment me."

After shouting at the ceiling and petulantly kicking her feet under the comforter Ocean pulled her blankets over her head and went back to sleep.

***

"Okay lady, I've had enough of you skulking around Seattle all by your lonesome. Tonight, we're going out for drinks and I'm gonna find you a man."

Jentri smiled across the table at Oceana and then smugly took a sip of her lemonade. Jentri was a Seattle native, eternal optimist and Oceana's best and only true friend she'd made since she moved… her only true friend ever in her life if she was truly being honest with herself. "Why is it that you think the whole of my future happiness hinges on me finding a man?"

Jentri chuckled and shook her head. "'Cause it does."

Knowing Jentri meant well Oceana gave her a teasing grin as she rolled her eyes at her. A romantic relationship was the farthest thing from her mind, she was comfortable being alone and more importantly she was used to being alone. In New York she'd grown accustomed to solitude, she was *Oceana Veritas Wade,* daughter of Maritza Giselle Wade, infamous seductress, femme fatale extraordinaire, money hungry succubus; and Oceana had lived her adolescent life feeling apologetic for her mother's sins. But here in Seattle she was just Ocean.

When she left New York, Ocean left her old self behind, she traded her former life of privilege and the self-loathing that came with it for calm, quiet, and carefree. Before she left the East Coast, all of her father's things had been boxed up and auctioned off to pay her mother's debts, and right as she was getting ready to bid the city adieu, she visited the law firm that had been handling the seizure so that she could pick up an unexpected but very welcomed settlement check, the very last of her father's estate. When she arrived at the law firm, she was none too pleased to find that in addition to the check, the overly presumptuous junior attorney had something else to give her. As soon as she entered his office, she was greeted by the attorney Mr. Cartridge, who in his right hand held her check, and in his left, his hard on.

She was used to men making assumptions about her virtue or lack there-of based on her mother's reputation, and in the past, she'd even been propositioned by some of her mother's old *benefactors* which really wasn't all that surprising, Maritza was beautiful but her beauty paled in comparison to Ocean's. Ocean's beauty rivaled that of a Greek Goddess, she had long, wavy, dark brown hair, big brown chestnut eyes and a smile that had this regal quality to it. And to top it all off, she had a body that women paid millions to get, and went broke trying to maintain.

While she was used to the inappropriate and uncomfortable advances of presumptuous men, that morning in Mr. Cartridges office she was officially exhausted and decided she had, had enough of all the lude and indecent proposals that continuously came her way. As Mr. Cartridge stood there smiling at her with her cashiers check in his right hand and his sex in his left, Ocean did the only thing she could think to do in that moment and she told him to *keep the money and go and fuck himself,* and then she left. As she walked down the hallway, she screamed at the top of her lungs how much she hated lawyers which drew the attention of the entire skeleton staff that was there.

In truth the money rightly belonged to her. Whether she choose to show her gratitude in sexual favors or not. Mr. Cartridge had no right to keep the check and eventually ended up mailing it to her after she arrived in Seattle. Along with the check came a brief apology note expressing his *sincerest* regrets for any possible miscommunication on his end at their final meeting.

Men like Mr. Cartridge were a dime a dozen, and the kind of men that Ocean always seemed to meet. Even in the office where she worked now, married lawyers winked and smiled at her all day long, it disgusted her.

"Ocean you're gorgeous. I seriously don't understand how you're single. I mean, if sexuality was a choice— I'd turn lesbian for you. I would, I swear. You don't even try to look good; you just wake up and done. No makeup, no primping no—you know, I don't think I've even ever seen you brush your hair. And then there's your clothes, you dress like a bum. You get up in the morning and throw on some moo moo looking shirt dress and brush your teeth and somehow, you're still my sexiest friend. It's not fair. You know what I'd be doing if I had your looks? I wouldn't be paying for shit anymore first of all, I'd be some rich guy's sugar baby. I'd be swimming in diamonds and pearls and jet setting. I'm telling you, you better use it or lose it 'cause looks don't last forever."

Thankfully Jentri's rant was interrupted by the sound of a guitar chord coming from Ocean's pocket. "Hello?"

"Ocean, I need you to come in today and get a brief together for me."

"Mr. Edwards?"

Jentri looked across the table smugly at Ocean and giggled and shook her head. "And if I had your looks, I definitely wouldn't be working some temp job, especially not for that arrogant asshole."

Ocean shook her head and smiled back at Jentri before returning her attention back to her unexpected caller.

"What time can you get here?"

"Mr. Edwards, today is Saturday, I don't work for you on weekends."

Annoyed by her reply Greg growled into the phone. "I know what day it is. What time can you get here? I need this brief together before Monday." Sensing her resistance to his request and with his ego which commanded that he not resort himself to pleading his need to her for her assistance, he decided on the next best thing. "Look, I'll pay you double for the day."

Ocean smiled, she found the precariousness of Greg's situation amusing, while she loathed being *desired* by the men in the building where she worked, she took extreme gratification in being *needed* by this particular man. As she quickly considered her options for the remainder of the day, she shrugged off her dislike of Greg, winked at Jentri and flashed her a quick smile. "Fine. I'll be there in an hour."

After contemplating how the rest of her day might go, despite her love for Jentri, she'd rather not spend the remainder of her day obsessing over men and what they could do for her. Another factor that helped her in making her final decision was the fact that she needed the money. The twenty-five thousand dollars that she'd gotten from her father's estate was nearly gone. While she didn't share her mother's lavish spending habits, she had inherited her father's exquisite taste for art and while her art purchases satisfied her soul, they didn't keep her warm and fed, so the opportunity to earn a little extra cash was a welcomed invitation.

CHAPTER THREE

With the holiday season rolling in, the legal office was starting to become quite busy. Two days earlier, after coming into work on her day off, Ocean and Greg had come to an agreement with her scheduling and she'd agreed to work one extra hour every day during the week until the New Year. The extra time was welcomed and, much to her delight, not something she had to ask for. While assisting Greg the past Saturday with one of his cases, when she was done, and on her way out of the office, from out of the corner of her eye she could see Greg cringe, so she paused; his obvious discomfort amused her because she knew that his reaction meant he needed something from her.

When he first approached her about extending her hours, she didn't respond right away. She let him twist in the wind for a moment for her own entertainment. She needed the money, so of course she'd work the extra hour but she enjoyed watching Greg twitch. So that day she dragged it out as long as she could and took pleasure in depositing the image of him in her memory bank. Despite the un-pleasantry of working extra hours with Greg, the arrangement meant she didn't need to cover for other temps in the building anymore, which she didn't mind as far as the work went, but the lawyers were another thing. They were always staring at her and flirting with her—these supposedly honest, principled, married men. In a way

Greg's dislike of her was somewhat comforting and she figured better the devil she knew.

That Monday morning Ocean had spent the entire morning fielding angry calls from clients wanting status reports on their cases as well as chatting up new clients who had walked in the office. By noon she was thankful to see Greg walking down the hallway.

"Mr. Edwards, I have several…"

Greg walked into the office straight past Ocean and her waiting area full of prospective clients and went straight into his office without saying a word.

The fact that Greg's waiting area was full which it never was should have delighted him, he should have been thrilled. As astonished as she was her appall by his behavior took front and center. Ocean gave the visitors in the waiting area her best *I'm sorry* smile then she quickly scooted from behind her desk and headed into Greg's office.

"That was rude."

Annoyed and confused Greg frowned at Ocean as he struggled to undo his tie. After flopping down in his seat, he quickly shook his head and shrugged his shoulders. "So, what's your point? I've had a hectic day, I don't have time for pleasantries. Who are they anyway? I don't have any appointments scheduled for today."

"That's no excuse to be rude and you were very rude. They're prospective clients, they wanted to see if you'd take on their cases. I personally don't think they all need lawyers but that's just me."

Greg laughed as he folded his arms and leaned back in his seat. "*You* don't think they need a lawyer? Well thank the Lord they didn't ask you. They came here to see me, right? Tell them I'll be with them in twenty minutes."

"Are you asking me to stay and wait with them?"

"Did you have somewhere else to be?"

Annoyed Ocean took a breath and slowly approached Greg's desk. "Lunch. I'd like to eat lunch. I've been here all alone all day answering phones and talking to walk-ins, I've barely had time to use the restroom and now it's half past twelve. I'd like to take my lunch."

Flagrantly disregarding the effort she had put in all day on his behalf, Greg flipped through the pile of memos Ocean had dropped on his desk. "It's not one o'clock yet. Your lunch is at one."

"No, my lunch is at twelve, I had something scheduled last week that required me to take my lunch at one, hence it being listed on the calendar, but my normal lunch schedule is from twelve to one. Do you not remember the hours you hired me for?"

Greg paid little to no attention to Ocean's increasing frustration as he continued to thumb through the numerous messages she'd given him. "Hey, what's this? Maxwell Prentiss called? What did he say?"

"I don't know, what does the message say he said?"

Stunned by the combativeness of her response Greg let the stack of memos in his hand fall to his desk. "Excuse me? What exactly is your problem? I know you think you've got me over a barrel and I won't fire you but let's get this straight, this is *my* office, you work for me and when I ask you a question I expect it to be answered in a professional manner and if you can't do that then you can go and tell the agency to place you somewhere else."

Gazes fixed on each other, Greg and Ocean squared off neither wanting to back down. Greg's reputation as a boss had both positives and negatives, he was an asshole but he paid really well, so…Ocean blinked.

Satisfied by her silent submission and feeling victorious Greg sat up straight and smiled at Ocean as he plucked a single memo from the pile laying on his desk. "Maxwell Prentiss…what did he say when he called?"

As she shut her eyes and inhaled deeply trying to calm herself, Ocean quickly replayed all the calls she had taken and tried to pinpoint the conversation in question. Once found, she slowly opened her eyes and met Greg's condescending stare.

"He asked if you were in...you weren't. He said to let you know that *Maxwell Prentiss* called and then he asked me if he and I had ever met before...we haven't."

"And?"

"And—that was it." As she turned to walk away, she was feeling much more annoyed with herself than she was with Greg. She'd overplayed her hand with Greg, she knew he needed her and she was the only one who'd been able to tolerate him beyond a week but now he knew that she needed him too. Before she could make it out of the room, she sighed at the sound of Greg's throat clearing which beckoned her to turn around. "Was there something else, Mr. Edwards?"

"Yes actually, there is. I'm going to have myself a quick snack. Please let the visitors in the waiting area know I'll be with them shortly and before you leave for lunch at one o'clock, go ahead and forward the phone to voicemail. That'll be all."

CHAPTER FOUR

The week seemed to drag on after the confrontation Ocean had, had with Greg on Monday. By Wednesday she was pained that it wasn't Friday, but she decided to continue to silently shoulder through the remainder of the work week; and ironically her new work hours were working against Greg. Much to his disadvantage, the one o'clock hour was the offices busiest hour, dozens of people were always calling in on their way back in to their jobs, and if they weren't calling, they were dropping by and very often in a hurry, trying to get a quick update on their case. Greg was completely swamped and overwhelmed but his pride wouldn't allow him to say so. His, and her, silence about the issue had become a staring contest of sorts and just like last time Greg refused to blink first no matter how much harder he had to work.

A week ago, Ocean had used her *requested* one o'clock lunch to attend an art auction downtown. Despite her new paycheck to paycheck lifestyle, she walked into the auction house confident and determined. While there were many things about her past life that she chose not to think about and desired to forget, the love she and her father shared for art was not one of them. Her father had once told her that his success, his architectural ingenuity and strength stemmed from his deep appreciation of art and he was happy to see that his love and respect had been passed on to Ocean, and he whole heartedly believed that it would serve her well.

Ocean wanted her father's artwork back, all of it would have been what she preferred but it would also be completely unrealistic considering her current circumstance. So instead, she decided to settle for whatever pieces she could afford, but only after she purchased the one piece she absolutely had to have. She never really understood the term *starving artist* until this year—not truly, but now...now she understood it and felt its hunger pains. She understood that there were some things in life that were so beautiful, so mesmerizing that it was worth it to go without eating. She understood that food would never fill her or make her feel the way she felt when she stood in front of artistic brilliance.

Since she arrived in Seattle, she hadn't had a single distinguishable feeling outside of relief from being out of New York and annoyance from working with Greg, she was just there in Seattle, living; but, she wasn't living as badly as she thought she'd be, but she also wasn't sure how she felt about any of it yet, if she felt anything at all. Then on the day of the auction she was overcome with emotion, she was completely filled with rage.

She attended the auction to buy back her favorite small pastel portrait that had hung in the study of her family's apartment for her entire childhood. The portrait was by her all-time favorite artist, Edgar Degas. There was something about Degas' tiny little dancers that resonated with her. The girls on the canvass were so beautiful, so admired yet looked so sad and so lonely. She had a certain understanding with the portrait and she wanted it back. More so than any other piece that had been taken she wanted this one piece. When the item finally came up for bid, she was so excited she nearly leapt out of her seat as it was unveiled to the audience. Her excitement proved to be short lived when she raised her paddle and smiled at the auctioneer whose eyes met hers but whose finger pointed at a man five rows ahead of her who also had his paddle in the air.

The male bidder five rows up proved not only to be quicker on the draw than she was but he also had more money. She lost the bid and she was pissed; and to make matters worse the wealthy, pompous asshole strutted up to her afterwards and attempted to flirt with her.

Completely disheartened Ocean slumped down in her chair and sulked. She hadn't noticed the handsome stranger approaching her until his black loafers were toe to toe with her red ballet flats. As soon as she looked up, he smiled and winked at her. "No need to be so put out about it. Ya win some, ya lose some. I'd be more than happy to let you have one final look at it, how about over lunch?"

In one effortless regal motion, Ocean rose to her feet never breaking her gaze from his and defiantly held her chin up in the air. "Go fuck yourself."

As she returned back to her desk that Wednesday afternoon, she smirked slightly to herself as she thought about the look on the man's face as she walked away from him. Served him right for the way he bid against her.

"Oceana, are you back from lunch?"

Despite how much she wished this week was over already and regardless of the fact that she had another ten minutes left of her lunch hour that day, Ocean decided not to be petty and instead she acknowledged Greg's question.

"Yes Mr. Edwards. Is there something you needed?"

"Step into my office, please."

Please, the man had actually said please without being prompted to do so, and to top it off there wasn't a hint of condescension in his tone.

"Yes, Mr. Edwards?" Ocean stood in the doorway of Greg's office cautiously optimistic as to what it was he had to say.

"Come in, please. Take a seat." Greg was visibly agitated and he looked exhausted as well but did his best to try and hide it. His hypnotic blue eyes looked sad and lonely today. "Listen, I'm going to be heading out of town to work on a case tomorrow morning, I

23

won't be back until Monday. I need you to come in a half hour early for the next two days to open and if you wouldn't mind closing up when you leave."

"Come in early? But I already stay late. Every day I stay late."

The irises of Greg's eyes were flat and despondent not at all what Ocean would have expected them to look like considering her resistance to his request.

"Yes, yes I know and I'm sorry it's such short notice but—"

Sensing there was a larger issue at play, Ocean sighed as she grabbed the door handle. "You know what, it's fine. I'll come in early and I'll leave even later, it's totally fine."

"Thank you, Oceana."

"You know, you can call me, Ocean. I prefer, Ocean."

"Yeah, thanks…Ocean. Thank you."

Due to her lack of friends, past and present tense, Ocean may not have had the best gauge on other people's emotions; after all, Jentri was her first real adult friend. Back in New York she led mostly a solitary lifestyle. She was the girl that parents whispered to their daughter to stay away from and turned their son's heads as she passed in the street. As a result of all her alone time she developed into somewhat of a socially awkward adult, which often times, quite by accident, translated as her being uncaring and tactless. Her manners were impeccable and no matter how hard she tried to fight it and be relaxed, she had an air of elegance about her at all times. But as far as common social skills went, a lot of the time social graces eluded her. But the one thing she could always see clearly was sorrow, and sorrow was what was all over Greg's face. As much as she didn't care for Greg, she didn't want him to feel *that*, she knew what that felt like and in that moment, she felt a little bit of it for him and with him.

"Mr. Edwards— are you all right?"

Greg sat behind his desk facing his computer but not really seeing it. He was off in a daze somewhere.

"Mr. Edwards?" Ocean cleared her throat loudly hoping that would help break the trance he was in. "Mr. Edwards?"

There was no response. Clearly Greg had already left the office and was off working on what one could only assume to be an emotionally draining case.

CHAPTER FIVE

"The whole thing was a mess. A real fucken mess. I mean if my family ever did that to me, I'd—I'd…I honestly don't know what the hell I'd do. They pretty much called him a nutcase."

"They're just worried Gregory. They just want to help."

Greg shook his head and sighed. Even in the comfort of his own home, the place where he could unwind and loosen up, he sat next to his fiancée, dressed as if he were headed into a press conference. His fiancée was no different. Amelia Elizabeth Walcott, like Greg was a successful attorney, only she was a corporate attorney. In the five years that she'd been practicing law she never once professionally argued in court. If it weren't for law school and mock trials, she likely wouldn't be able to navigate her way around the inside of a courtroom if she tried. Amelia was driven even though she hadn't worked as hard as Greg to get where she was, she was relentless in her efforts to maintain the position that she'd inherited. And in doing so she left many a wounded party in her wake. Greg admired that about her.

Amelia didn't let anyone or anything stand in her way. It was she who often stood in the way of others and she took great pride in looking her best as she did so. She was never dressed in less than several thousand dollars' worth of jewelry, her heels were never under six hundred dollars, her outfits were always form-fitting, well-tailored and pressed to perfection. This Sunday evening Amelia sat beside Greg wearing a red Givenchy dress with a pair of Cartier earrings pillowed gently on her earlobes and a matching necklace which rested easily on her collarbone.

Greg was no slouch either, it was like the two were dressed to impress each other…impress or *out do*, it could be alleged that neither knew the difference. While Amelia had come from money and was used to certain kinds of extravagances, be it clothing, jewelry, automobiles, what have you; Greg grew up without any of it but enjoyed outshining those who had dined on these things, fed from the silver spoons people like him used to polish.

Greg learned his appearance could open doors for him at an early age. It could get him things and take him places. He'd grown up poor. He often went to school in raggedy hand-me-down clothing and with an empty stomach, but he'd learned quickly that his surprising blue eyes, dark features and coy smile were qualities not so easily overlooked. People wanted to help the *poor pitiful looking kid with the brilliant blue eyes*. They wanted to feed him and give him clothes and pocket money. Now, as a man, it wasn't pity Greg wanted but respect. His eyes, once soft and alluring, were now just as striking with contempt and conviction as they were in color and appearance.

This evening Greg's charcoal grey Calvin Klein suit that he wore with a black silk shirt only added to the contrast and distinction between his dark features and crystal-like eyes. And not to be outdone on the bling, his Tiffany & Co. cufflinks sparkled in the dim light of the living room eclipsing Amelia's shine.

"They just want his money, it's all they want Amelia. They just want to help themselves to his money. The entire case was complete bullshit."

"Gregory, think about it from their point of view. I mean be honest, it sounds a little crazy to me too."

Greg stood up and smoothed down his suit jacket and downed the rest of his Scotch. "HE'S NOT CRAZY."

In that moment Amelia was both delighted that she had gotten a rise out of Greg but also a little intimidated by his response, and in addition to that she found herself very aroused by his outburst and quickly got to her feet so that she might continue to exploit Greg's emotions in closer proximity.

With her body pressed firmly against his and her fingers firmly gripping a decent chunk of his black locks, Amelia smiled at him as she slowly twisted her hips into his pelvis.

"Gregory, let's not fight. We haven't seen each other in days and the last thing I want to do right now is fight with you." That was a lie. *Fighting* was the one thing the two of them did best. Even in the bedroom they fought, neither wanting to take the submissive role, both wanting to be on top. Sex with them was always hard, fast and aggressive, their bodies twisting and slapping against each other trying to get the upper hand, trying to make the other one cry out in ecstasy. It was quite the spectacle and they both loved it.

"Take off your dress."

Not one who cared too much for being told what to do Amelia stretched her body up against the length of his and took a quick nip at Greg's earlobe. "Make me." As she brought her weight back down on the heels of her Christian Louboutin's, she took the end of his Greg's tie between her fingers and gave it a firm tug, and just like that...the fight was on.

CHAPTER SIX

"We really need to figure out a better lunch schedule for you. I'm getting slammed everyday with client calls and people stopping by wanting to check the status of their case. That's *your* job."

Ocean bit back the retort that was begging to be released from her lips. She'd already tried her luck once before and Greg had called her bluff, and unbeknownst to him she too was on the agencies short list as far as placements went. Since she started with the temp agency, she'd been told her services were no longer needed from no less than eleven placements. Before starting with Greg she'd been duly advised that he was on his last leg with temps and she was on her last leg with placements; no one wanted to work with either of them so they two had better make it work for each other's sake.

"Oceana."

Ocean huffed and forced a smile as she tried to calm herself. She hated the way Greg said her name, it was condescending and with an air of *knowing*, which he didn't... he didn't know her. He didn't know anything about her.

"Mr. Edwards?"

"Do you have anything to say?"

"About lunch, Sir? Well, if you'd like, I can go back to my normal twelve o'clock lunch hour—you know, if that would help you."

Greg was less than amused by Ocean's obvious attempt to make him admit his error in judgement but rather than fight with someone he considered to be his intellectual inferior he ignored her comment all together.

"Clearly the hours between twelve and two are the busiest so I don't think you should take lunch at all during this time. I'm moving your lunch to two o'clock."

"I came in at eight a.m. I don't leave until six p.m. you've already changed my lunch once before, less than thirty days ago in fact and then you extend my schedule by an hour each day *and* let's not forget I came in early for you just last week and now you're telling me you're changing my schedule yet again?"

"Yes. Is that a problem Oceana?"

"OCEAN!"

"Excuse me?"

"Nothing, just—forget it."

Ocean was livid. She couldn't believe that just a few days ago she was feeling bad for him but now, now she wanted to punch him right in the nose, and the way he said her name *Oceana*—he didn't know her.

The expression on Ocean's face said everything her mouth did not, which greatly amused Greg who unintentionally laughed in her face, which only infuriated Ocean even more. For the first time since she started working there this was the first time she'd seen a sincere smile on Greg's face. She'd been waiting to see that man smile since she started. She honestly wasn't even sure if he knew how to smile. She never fathomed that the first time he'd show any genuine feelings of happiness and joy it would be to mock her.

With both her cheeks now looking as if they'd been smacked repeatedly for the past ten minutes and her bottom lip so red from anxiously biting at it, so red that it looked as if it were bleeding; Ocean took several deep short breaths in, in an effort to try and calm herself... it didn't work.

"Go straight to hell, you condescending sadistic son of a bitch." As much as she needed a job, she needed not to have to deal with this level of bullshit even more. Ocean stomped out of Greg's office went back to her desk and snatched her purse out of the bottom drawer and left the office.

Allowing his arrogance to get the better of him, Greg didn't follow after Ocean or call her after she stormed out, a decision he greatly regretted two hours later when he found himself with a waiting area full of clients, every line on his phone on hold and one of the firm's partners standing in his doorway.

"What in the hell is going on here, Edwards? Where's your assistant?" Leland Collins stood red faced in Greg's door, waiting for an explanation. Of all the senior partners at his firm Greg disliked Leland the most and since all the other partners disliked Greg, Leland was usually the one they sent to *check in on things*.

Collins, Pratt & Sink LLC was a small family friendly firm. The majority of their staff were extremely personable and empathetic to their client's needs, Greg was the complete opposite of the people he worked for and with. For Greg, it wasn't about empathy, it was about capital, closing cases and building his reputation. In truth, Greg hated the people he worked for, he thought they were soft, silly and irrational but they were the only firm that would hire him.

While none of the partners at the firm liked Greg, they tolerated him and to a certain degree they respected his work ethic. Greg was meticulous, relentless and had a fire in him like no one else there but the downside was that he was cold, dismissive and arrogant. The firm had only hired him because one of their existing clients, a very good client, put in a good word for him and mentioned how they might finally get the one client they'd been after for years just by taking Greg on.

Overwhelmed and short on patience Greg cut his piercing blue eyes at Leland then quickly put his head back down and continued shuffling through the stack of cases on his desk.

"I'm working Mr. Collins, what does it look like is going on, Sir?"

"And where is Ocean? Don't tell me you ran her off too?"

Leland waited for Greg to respond but he didn't. Growing impatient Leland slapped the door handle and stamped his foot on the carpet. "Edwards!"

"Yes, sir?"

"Where's Ocean?"

"She left, sir."

"So, you ran off another one?" Leland shook his head in disgust and sharply sucked his teeth. "You get her back here, Edwards. This firm is not going to be known for treating its employees badly and running them off all because of you. You get her back here. Apologize for whatever it was that you said and I don't care how right you were or what you think about her, you apologize and ask her to come back."

After Leland had gone and shut the door behind him Greg stopped looking through the stack of files on his desk and sat down in his seat and took a deep breath.

CHAPTER SEVEN

"Don't get me wrong, I'm glad you decided to come out and *finally* let those luscious locks of yours down but did it have to be tonight? There isn't much going on, on a Monday night."

Ocean looked at Jentri and smiled as she nodded her head back and forth to the acoustic soul pumping out the speakers in the dimly lit bar. "I don't care, I need this." Ocean downed the shot of tequila then scanned the semi deserted bar. After making eye contact with a cute but not overly attractive or overly dressed guy sitting alone in a booth across the room, Ocean leaned closer to Jentri. "What do you think about him?"

Jentri curled the left side of her lip in contemplation and quickly tilted her head from side to side. "Uh—I think you could do better. Much better. I mean, he's okay but he doesn't look like he's got much going for him; no suit and tie, no bling and his shoes—they're not even shoes they're sandals. He's not bad looking but you could definitely do better. Think *Armani* not *Abercrombie*."

Ocean quickly signaled the bartender to bring another round of shots then she quickly turned her attention back to *Mr. Abercrombie* who was still staring at her and smiling in her direction. Ocean smiled back and tilted her head beckoning him to come and join them.

Jentri let out a loud exasperated sigh and rolled her eyes. "Seriously Ocean? You'll be lucky if he can even afford to pick up our tab tonight. By the way, you might wanna take it easy on the tequila, that's your fifth shot."

"Sixth."

"What?"

"It's my sixth shot."

"Well then maybe you should just stop instead of slowing down."

"Lighten up Jentri, I'm having a good time and aren't you always telling me I should get out more and learn to enjoy life?"

"Yeah, but…"

"But, nothing. I'm out, I'm enjoying myself, there's not *butts* about it."

An hour and a half later, after two Margaritas and some pleasant small talk, Ocean closed her bar tab, ordered a very reluctant Jentri into her own cab home, and then she left the bar to get better acquainted with the man whose name she'd already forgotten.

***

Frightened from her sleep by the sound of guitar chords, Ocean jolted into an upright position panicked and confused. After realizing that it was just her cell phone she began to calm down a bit; but before her heart had reached its normal resting rate again, it was sent a flutter when she looked around trying to locate her cell and realized she wasn't home. She had no idea where she was. Again, the guitar chord struck panic into her heart and she quickly got out of bed and ran across the room to the pile of clothing on the floor she recognized to be her own and she searched for her cell.

"Hello?" Ocean did her best to whisper as she tiptoed her naked body around in circles desperately searching for her underwear as she tried not to wake the naked man whose name she couldn't remember and whose face was buried in the pillow next to the one she recently abandoned.

"Oceana Wade!" Jentri's high pitched scream hit Ocean's ear drum like an icepick. "Are you crazy? Are you okay? I've been up worried half to death thinking that you left with some psychotic strangler who cut you into pieces then used you as bait and threw you into an ocean."

"Well, that's a bit much, don't you think? And if he's a strangler, why is he cutting me into pieces? Why not just, you know—strangle me?" Finally finding her lace black panties which had somehow ended up covering a picture frame which held a photo of whom she could have only guessed was the naked man's girlfriend, no, there was a ring on her finger, not girlfriend, *fiancée*. The two looked really happy. Ocean pulled up her panties and looked over at the man sleeping peacefully and shook her head at him.

"Oceana Wade! This is not funny. I just told Jeff if I didn't hear from you by this morning I was gonna call SWAT."

"SWAT? Really, Jentri?"

"Oceana—"

"Enough with the given name nonsense. I'm fine... I have no idea where I am, but I'm fine. In fact, I'm better than fine. In one night I got to blow off some steam *and* re-confirm to myself that single life ain't half bad." Ocean quickly glimpsed at the happy couple in the photo again and then back at the bed. "It's certainly better than the alternative."

"It wasn't good, huh?"

"Can't say it was bad but it definitely wasn't memorable."

"So, what was it then? Beer googles—I'm sorry, *tequila goggles* come off?"

Ocean studied the smiling face gazing adoringly at the woman with the princess cut engagement ring on her finger. "No, no he's not bad looking. Actually, I think he's kind of cute."

"So, what the problem?"

"The problem is, is that he looks downright adorable in the picture on his dresser of him and his fiancée."

"No—"

"Yes."

"Oh my God, Ocean you need to get out of there."

"I know."

"Like right now."

"I know."

"What if she walks in? Oh my God, Ocean this is so bad."

"I know, I know, believe me, I know. I'm getting dressed right now."

"Where is he?"

"He's still in bed sleeping. Hold on Jentri, I've got another call coming in." Ocean quickly looked down at her caller ID before switching over. It was the law office calling.

"Hello?"

"Oceana, good morning." Greg cleared his throat. "I hope I didn't wake you?"

"No."

"Good." There was a long uncomfortable pause on the line before Greg's throat clearing once again took center stage. "Oceana, I was hoping you and I could clear the air with each other and you could come in and get back to work?"

Suddenly her day was looking up. Ocean stopped dressing and stood in her bra and panties smiling like a cat with a mouse caught between its paws. As she stood there proudly basking in her victory, her mood suddenly took a dive when she heard the rumbling of the sheets from across the room. *Mr. Abercrombie* was awake and was *very* happy to see her. "Damn. You look even hotter sober."

"Greg cleared his throat again. "Sorry, am I interrupting something?"

Ocean quickly bent down and grabbed her pants off the floor and began putting them on. "No, you're not, that was just my—never mind, you're not interrupting. So, you were saying something about clearing the air?"

"Yes. I know you and I didn't end the day yesterday on the best of terms."

"You mean when I quit?"

"When you left. Anyway, now that we've both had some time to think things over calmly, I was hoping we could move past yesterday's event and start fresh?"

"So, you're asking me to come back to work?"

"Yes."

"Okay."

"Okay?"

"Yes."

"So, what time should I expect you in this morning?"

"I've gotta run home and change so I'll be in after lunch... at one o'clock."

Greg sighed. "See you at one."

***

Outside Greg's door, Ocean smiled to herself as she smoothed down her powder blue poplin button up. As she tapped gently at the door, she took a confident breath and gave her head full of curls a casual shake.

"Come in."

"Mr. Edwards." Ocean paused at the half open door. "Oh, sorry, I didn't realize you were with a client. I just wanted to let you know I was here and I'll be at my desk if you need me."

Ocean smiled at the man sitting across from Greg and offered a friendly wave.

"Thank you, Oceana."

As she turned to leave, she was halted by the stranger whose hand was now raised in her direction signaling her to stay. "Now Greg, where are your manners? You haven't introduced us." The handsome stranger slowly made his way over to Ocean and extended his hand. "Allow me. I'm Maxwell Prentiss."

Ocean smiled and took Max's hand. "Nice to meet you. I'm—"

Max chuckled. "I know who you are, Mademoiselle Degas"

Recognition flooded Ocean and her jaw dropped. "You're— you're the— You stole my painting."

"Well no, I didn't *steal* it, I purchased it. I outbid you."

Ocean's face turned a deep shade of red as she stared contentiously at Max and she tried to stop the myriad of insults that were burning her throat from escaping her mouth.

Confused Greg rose from his seat and casually buttoned his suit jacket. "You two have already met?"

Max turned to Greg and smiled and then turned back towards Ocean and winked. "Yeah, we've met. This is the pretty little thing I told you about, the one I ran into at the auction."

Greg stepped around his desk and stuck his hands in his pockets as he slowly approached the two. "The woman who blew you off?"

His eyes still fixed on Ocean and his smile growing wider by the minute, Max took a small step forward purposely invading Ocean's personal space. "Yes, she would be the one. If I remember correctly, I believe she told me—"

Unfazed by his bodily intrusion, Ocean stared up at Max with confidence and resentment. "I told you to go fuck yourself."

"That's right, you did."

Still confused and now very much annoyed Greg shook his head and threw his hands up in the air. "What the hell is going on here?" Greg looked at Ocean and raised an eyebrow. "Oceana, you think you could get back to work, *please*."

Surprised that he wasn't asking her to leave permanently after the exchange she just had with a client, Ocean nodded and quickly turned around to leave but she was once again halted by Max who gently placed his hand on the top of hers as she tried to shut the door.

"Mademoiselle Degas, you're welcomed to come and view *my* portrait anytime you wish. I'd love to have you over anytime."

CHAPTER EIGHT

"Absolutely not." Greg leaned over the pool table and took his shot and missed his mark by quite a distance. "Damn it! You're doing this on purpose."

"I'm not doing anything. You just suck at pool. You can't *pretty boy* yourself out of this."

"Go to hell."

Max laughed as he struck the cue ball and sunk the final two solid balls into the right corner pocket. "Two down one more to go and by the way, I haven't got the time today to go to hell, I've got plans later on... I'll be on the phone with your assistant." Max looked up from the table and smiled. "Eight ball, corner pocket." One deliberate stroke of the pool-stick and the eight ball was sunk exactly where Max said it would be. "I'll take that number from you now."

Greg scowled at Max and shook his head as he plopped down on the stool behind him. "Let's have a drink first."

"Why? You afraid I'm gonna abandon you after you give me the number?"

Greg ignored Max's last comment and turned to the waitress and put in a drink order. Sensing Greg was getting bent out of shape Max decided it might be best to go easy on him, easy but not back off. As he reset the pool table, he began to whistle the theme from pretty woman. "Come on Greg, lighten up. What's the big deal anyway? You got a thing for her?"

"Fuck no."

"Then why do you give a shit?"

"She's my assistant."

"She's your temp."

"Not according to Leland."

"Is that what this is about, Leland? Don't worry about Leland, I can take care of him."

"You're not fucking my assistant."

"Why not?"

"Because."

"Because why?"

"Damn it, Max. Why can't you just find somebody else? Anybody else."

"I mean, I guess I could but I kinda like how much this is pissing you off. Just give me a reason, a *real* reason why you don't want me to see her."

Relieved the waitress had returned with the whiskey he'd ordered, Greg took a big gulp and grabbed the waitress by the elbow before she had a chance to flee. "I'll have another please. Neat, this time."

Max stood in front of the pool table his hazel brown eyes fixed on Greg. "I'm waiting."

"Go ahead and break."

"You know what I meant dipshit. Give me a reason."

Greg swallowed the last of the whiskey in his glass then picked up his pool-stick again and made his way back over to the table. "She works for me and you're my client. It's just not appropriate."

"Not appropriate?" Max scoffed and shook his head before leaning over to take his shot. "That's bullshit and you know it. Stop dicking around and tell me the truth."

Now his turn, Greg leaned over to take his shot then quickly stood back up and glared at Max. "What the hell is that supposed to mean?"

"You know exactly what I mean."

Greg stomped back over to the table where the waitress had left the glass of whiskey he'd requested then he threw back the entire glass. "That was a cheap shot. You know I did what I did to survive. You're just looking for entertainment. There's a big difference." After regaining his composure Greg walked back over to the table as confidently as he could and leaned down to take his next shot, which ended up being a scratch.

Max laughed and ran his fingers through his hair. "See there, God doesn't like liars. You've done some less than appropriate things throughout your life when you didn't *have to*, you know I would never call you out for doing what you *needed* to do and you know that better than anyone, brother."

Greg threw his pool-stick on the table and skulked back over to his stool. "Fine, you want a reason? Here's a reason, I can't stand her. If Leland wasn't forcing me to keep her, I'd fire her ass. She's whiny and needy and mouthy and God, is she arrogant."

"And she's gorgeous, smart and sweet—well not to me, *not yet* anyway, but I saw the way she interacts with your clients and she's very sweet. Maybe you just bring out the worst in her. I mean, *clearly* she's got a knack for bringing out the petty in you." Max slowly strolled over to the empty stool by Greg and grabbed his now watery whiskey and took a seat. "You can text me her number later." Max lifted his glass in salutation then took a sip. "Anyway, how's Amelia?

"Amelia's great."

"That's all?"

"What ese is there? You asked how she was and I told you."

"Yes, you did, very matter of fact like indeed." Max grinned and shook his head as he swallowed the last of the whiskey in his glass.

"What the hell did you want me to say? You want me to say she's doing bad?"

"No, no not at all. It's just— never mind."

Greg frowned and shoved Max on the shoulder. "Bullshit never mind, *it's just* what? Say it. You don't like her. Go ahead, say it."

"That's not what I was going to say."

"But it's what you were thinking."

Max scoffed and reached for the basket of tortilla chips on the table. "It's not that I don't like her, it's just I don't like her for you. I think you could do better."

"Better than Amelia? Better how? She's perfect. She graduated *cum laude*, she comes from a great family, she's on the fast track to partner at a very prestigious firm; she's smokin' hot and I mean, what else is there?"

"Intrigue, excitement, compassion, fire. Should I go on?"

Overcome with laughter Greg immediately dismissed the sincerity of Max's response. "And you believe there's a woman out there who has all this? Who has all of Amelia's best qualities and then some?" Greg let a burst of air ripple out from his lips as he rolled his eyes at Max. "What do you know? You're single and if you're looking for a woman like that, that's why you're single. That kind of woman doesn't exist."

Max shook off Greg's mocking and popped a tortilla in his mouth as he reached into his pocket for his cell phone. "Yes, I am single, I'm glad you brought that up." Max smiled at Greg and cleared his throat. "Ocean's number please."

His effort to avoid giving Max Ocean's phone number had proven to be fruitless. He'd hoped by not talking about it that Max would just forget, but unfortunately, he hadn't and now Greg was annoyed once again. "One more game? You win and I'll give you the number."

"Are you forgetting I already won? Twice."

Greg reached for his pool-stick and offered Max a sly grin. "I'll put in a good word for you too, how about that?"

"A good word from you? I thought she didn't like you. Besides I don't need a wingman, I'm great with women."

"Oh yeah I forgot *Mademoiselle Degas*." Greg threw his hands up in confusion as he frowned at Max. "What the hell were you doing buying a Degas for anyway? You're not even into that kind of art, you're more Salvador Dali than Edgar Degas."

Max grabbed the pool-stick and made his way to the end of the table to break smiling to himself the whole way there. "That's true. I'm not into Degas. I only bought the painting because I saw she wanted it and I want her and now I've got something she wants."

"And what exactly is it you want with her? Clearly more than a one-night stand, you're buying artwork and showing up at my office just to talk to her, you want something more than just one night."

As the balls clacked against each other and rolled around the felt top of the pool table Max nodded and smiled to himself. "Her. I want her. I want to know her. I need to find out why it is just the thought of her makes me smile. I mean—how does she do that?"

CHAPTER NINE

"Are you excited? Tell me you're excited?"

Ten o'clock Saturday morning walking around the pricy side of the city in the damp air was not a good time to Ocean, it in fact did the opposite of excite her. "I'm ecstatic. This is my happy face, can't you tell?"

Unlike Ocean, Jentri was absolutely thrilled. The day had finally arrived for her to try on her custom-made wedding dress.

"Ocean, I can't wait for you to see it, it's gorgeous. You're gonna die."

"Death by dress?"

"You joke but you just wait, this gown is gonna take your breath away. It is positively stunning."

Amused by Jentri's excitement, Ocean cracked her first smile of the day. She knew before she saw it that the gown would be stunning just like Jentri said it would be, but the whole fuss of wedding dresses was something she never really understood. To purposely spend what could be a down payment on a car or a house on a dress that you intentionally bought to wear just once was completely impractical to her. Then again, she didn't understand a lot about the world she grew up in. "So, how much is this gown setting you back?"

Confused by why she would ever think to ask such a frivolous question, Jentri shook her head and frowned. "Hell if I know. It's not about the money anyway, this gown is a work of art. Whatever Jeff has to pay for it I promise you it's well worth it."

The boutique they arrived at looked as pretentious as Ocean thought it would. You couldn't just walk into the shop, *heavens no*, you had to ring a bell to get in because God forbid any vagrants or middle-class folk wander in and attempt to browse.

The inside of the boutique had wall to wall creamy Berber carpeting, the walls were a shimmery champagne color and the lighting was bright enough to compete with the sun that day. Considering the boutique was dedicated solely to wedding gowns Ocean was surprised to find that there weren't as many in the store as she thought there would, or should be. As she looked at the empty spaces where she thought racks should have been Ocean swiveled her head around and frowned until she landed on the Botox infused plastered smile of the sales associate. "Are these all the dresses you have?" The stone-faced associate glared at her with dull blue eyes and blinked slowly in irritation. "*We deal in quality over quantity.*" The associate looked her up and down in disapproval, her silence a clear message that Ocean was to keep her grubby unpolished hippie hands off their fine things. Not only was the shop short on wedding gowns but it wasn't exactly bursting with *wedding joy* either.

Standing confidently in her boyfriend-styled denims and her heather grey oversized sweat shirt Ocean raised both eyebrows and smiled. She was not about to have this woman make her flee from the store, she was feeling very *Pretty Woman* in her ballet slippers and casual comfy clothing and just like the interaction Julia had with her rude sales associate, Ocean knew this woman worked on commission as well... big mistake. "*Quality*. It's funny you should say that because I looked around and I don't see too many items in here with a value of more than six thousand dollars. Also, several of the *big names* in the wedding gown biz appear to be absent from your closets. Is that why you had to ship her dress out? You don't have the *quantity* to cover the cost to keep an onsite seamstress to work on your *quality* gowns?"

Insulted and clearly flustered, the sales associate quickly smoothed down her blouse and quickly turned and snapped her head in the direction of the backroom. "If you'll excuse me Ms. McDavid, I'll go retrieve your gown for you now."

Intrigued by Ocean's remarks to the clerk Jentri slowly circled Ocean staring at her with both skepticism and admiration. "You got something you wanna tell me?"

Despite her love for Jentri, Ocean had decided not to confide in her all the details of her past. Jentri didn't know anything about *Oceana Veritas Wade* and Ocean loved her all the more just for that. Realizing she tipped her hand slightly she coyly smiled at Jentri as she strolled her way over to the love seat by the mirrored viewing area. "Tell you what?"

"Uh—tell me how you, *Bargain Basement Betty* of all people, *you* know about the *big names* in the wedding gown industry."

Having been dragged to numerous weddings by her mother who was always on the hunt for another benefactor after Ocean's father died, she'd seen her fair share of overpriced gowns, she knew the designer names the brides *wanted*, the ones they'd settle for and the ones they'd been forced to take. Being able to recognize the difference had become somewhat of a game for her, a game that she was very good at. "It's not like I live under a rock, Jentri. I know the difference between pretty and stunning. I also know how much it cost to be stunning and for those lucky enough to afford stunning, I know they want to see names like Siriano, de la Renta, or Westwood. I may not know a lot about fashion but I know about art and their designs are artistic masterpieces. If I had money, I'd buy one of their dresses—not to wear but to display in my apartment as artwork."

"You know, I believe you would do some crazy shit like that; and you'd probably walk down the aisle in some Punky Brewster inspired monstrosity."

"Probably so, I think the girl had vison."

"Now that is a vison!" As the sales associate carried in Jentri's dress with the help of another assistant, Jentri stood anxiously with a smile so wide plastered on her face it made Ocean's cheeks red.

Ocean sat quietly and listened to Jentri hum in excitement as she got dressed near the viewing area which had been sectioned off by three large antique looking fabric dividers. Despite her clear disinterest in today's events she was secretly excited to see her friend in bridal couture.

"Okay Ocean, are you ready? You're gonna die. It's amazing.

"It—is—something." Ocean was shocked. She'd expected the dress to be a bit extravagant but she hadn't expected it to be just downright ugly. As she slowly circled Jentri who stood beaming atop the viewing room platform Ocean desperately searched for something to say.

It's gorgeous, right? You love it? Tell me you love it." Jentri was bouncing so much in excitement that her nipples began to escape the top of the gown.

The dress was tragically overdone. Behind blush puffs of taffeta there was powder blue lace trim which rested beneath ivory silk draping that needlessly covered her arms and left her breast completely exposed. In addition to the pounds of waring fabric twisted into the shape of a dress; there were gaudy oversized rhinestones awkwardly placed around what Ocean assumed must have been the neckline. The dress was a disaster.

"It's breathtaking Jentri. Are you sure you wanna show that much cleavage? You might distract the minister to the point where he forgets the words to the service."

"You think?" This of course was not a real negative for Jentri rather it was a validation of how good she looked. Jentri proudly posed in the mirror and flirted with her reflection. "Don't worry Ocean, I didn't put you in one of those typical tacky maid of honor dresses either, I mean your dress isn't custom made but it's cute."

Thankfully before she could respond she was saved by the soulful strum of a guitar sound coming from her pocket. "Hello?"

"Hi, Ocean?"

"Yeah?"

"Hi, it's Maxwell Prentiss. How are you?"

"Um—I'm okay." At least with the unexpected phone call Ocean now had a valid reason to show the confusion she was feeling inside outwardly on her face. "What can I do for you Mr. Prentiss? Wait... how did you get my number?"

"Call me Max, please. I got your number from Greg."

"Mr. Edwards gave you my personal number?"

"Yeah, Greg's a good friend of mine so when I asked, he was happy to help."

"I'm sure he was."

Completely taken with the sincerity of her response Max couldn't help but laugh. "Yeah, actually he wasn't too thrilled about it."

"So, what can I do for you, Max?"

"Well, I was hoping you'd take me up on my offer about coming over to see the painting and of course if you did, it would only be right to sit down afterwards and have a drink and discuss your thoughts on Degas' work. And, because it's been proven you should never drink on an empty stomach, we should also have a bite to eat while we have drinks and discuss art"

He was quite the crafty conversationalist and Ocean couldn't deny she was intrigued. "I do want to see the painting again." Ocean was no fool she was very aware he could care less if she saw the painting he just wanted to see her; and while she was adamantly opposed to becoming anything resembling a sugar baby, she decided that dinner and a drink could be a way to convince Max to sell her that which was taken from her… at a discounted rate of course. She would just have to make sure she had the conversation of her life to make it happen. "So, is tonight good for you?"

"Every night is good for me. I can come pick you up around eight if that's good for you?"

"Eight is perfect but just text me the address and I'll take a cab over."

"Sure thing. See you tonight."

"See you then." And so, it was game on. Tonight she would get what she wanted using her wit rather than her wiles and she was looking forward to it.

"Did I just hear you make a date with someone?" Jentri stared at Ocean in the viewing mirror. It was the first time since she stepped on the pedestal that she wasn't gawking at herself.

Ocean shrugged and smiled at Jentri as she coolly crossed her arms and leaned back against the love seat. "Maybe so."

CHAPTER TEN

"Your place is really nice, not what I was expecting but really, really nice." Ocean scanned the beautifully decorated walls of Max's townhome. The place was large, as she expected it to be, but it wasn't showy or pretentious in the least. To her surprise and extreme pleasure the townhome was lovely and welcoming.

As soon as she stepped foot in the door, she was met with a beautifully hand painted replica of the Roman Ruins. Had the hallway she entered been wider she would have sworn she was there in real life; and things only got better from there. The entire living room area had been carefully and artfully decorated around Michelangelo's painting *The Creation of Adam*, just the two touching fingertips, it was jaw dropping. In the kitchen, which had been set as a small French bistro, it made you feel as if you were sitting on some semi deserted cobblestone street far away from Seattle, Washington.

Normally, advances from men like Max, wealthy men, were unwelcomed and rejected but tonight Ocean couldn't help but feel a little flattered by Max who was clearly excited to see her. Max hadn't stopped smiling since he opened the door to let her in.

"I hope you didn't have any trouble finding the place, I know some cabbies can get a bit turned around by the way the street signs are numbered."

If she hadn't just walked in and spent the better part of her day with Jentri wedding shopping Ocean would have sworn she was drunk. She gently touched the wall; she was in complete awe of how skillfully done everything was and she wanted to confirm she hadn't gone crazy and she wasn't dreaming. Max's question fell on deaf ears, she was completely transfixed.

"The artist who painted for me is amazing. If you dream it, he can paint it. You can have his number if you want." Max handed Ocean a glass of Merlot as he slowly leaned in closer to her. "He's good, but he's no Degas."

She'd completely forgotten all about the Degas portrait she'd come over to con Max out of. "Oh yeah, I almost forgot." The merlot… the freaken' Merlot, she usually passed when offered Merlot or any other red wine, she preferred Sauvignon Blanc, but this Merlot, it was outstanding. Sipping and turning, her eyes searched each inch of the bistro but the Degas portrait was nowhere to be found, but the Merlot tasted so good and she was so relaxed and so captivated that she didn't even care.

Pleased with the evenings start and optimistic about how it would continue Max extended his arm to Ocean. "Mademoiselle, this way please." With arms linked and her hand softly resting on his bicep Max slowly led the way to the room that housed the catalyst for their meeting this evening. "You look gorgeous by the way."

Truth was Max would have thought Ocean looked outstanding in whatever she had on but this evening she had dressed for the occasion.

"Thank you. I'm feeling slightly overdressed though. I didn't expect you to…to…"

"Look like I just woke up?"

"Look so relaxed. I like it." Ocean didn't own too many clothing items that she considered *fancy*, she did however hold on to a dress or two to break out when the situation called for it, and tonight she thought she just might be in such a situation. This evening she traded her comfy loose-fitting Woodstock inspired attire for a cobalt blue knee length dress which she paired with some black Manolo Blahniks and a pair of chandelier earrings. She was completely uncomfortable but she looked good; despite his casual dress, so did Max.

Suits and ties and expensive labels didn't impress Ocean the way it did some other women. Even in his distressed blue jeans with the label ripped off and his nameless V-neck cotton grey shirt any woman would have found Max attractive. He had sandy blond hair a mischievous yet sheepish smile, and whiskey-colored eyes; even at his worst he still looked better than most men at their best. He also appeared to be in decent shape, he didn't look as if he frequented the gym on a daily basis, he wasn't overly muscular and his skin wasn't stretched to the point where it looked translucent from trying to cover them; but he didn't have the squishiness and squidge of your average couch potato, either. He was effortlessly handsome.

"I'm sorry, I wasn't trying to be rude or anything, you just seem like a pretty upscale kind of guy. I wasn't expecting you to be so casual. I like it. I wish I would have known." Ocean pulled at the sides of the dress and frowned as the spandex resisted her tugging.

"Well, feel free to get comfortable if you want. Kick off your heels, let your hair down and relax. I'm all about comfort over style."

Before they made it to the end of the hall Ocean was out of her heels and her hair was down.

Max looked down and grinned. "You still look absolutely amazing."

Inches shorter and with her hair now unrestrained, Ocean felt at ease. "Wow! This is spectacular. I seriously could not have dreamed of a better place for this portrait to be."

At the end of the hallway off to the left, away from all the other rooms in the townhome, in a room that was more than a library but a little less than a lounge, hung the Degas portrait that Ocean yearned to see. The room was large and spacious yet warm and inviting. The focal point of the room was the large hand-crafted bookshelf that took up the entire length of one of the walls and was built from floor to ceiling. The bookshelf was gorgeous, destressed wood with large spaces cut out at different points and its design appeared to be somewhat of a wave pattern and at its swell right in the center nestled amongst various literary geniuses was her Degas portrait. If she hadn't known when he had purchased the portrait, she would have sworn the shelf had been built around it, it looked very much at home where it was.

"So, what do you think?" As Max slowly crossed behind Ocean and made his way over to the big cushiony brown sofa on the other side of the room he stared back at Ocean, his whiskey eyes glistening with anticipation. "I hung it myself. I was going to put it in the living room but I thought she looked better in here."

Ocean was in awe of how perfect the painting looked exactly where it was, for her art wasn't just about the picture it was about everything; the surroundings the feeling, all of it. She felt as if she were standing before a true masterpiece in that moment and suddenly, she was hit with a touch of sadness. As much as she didn't want to admit she didn't have a place in her apartment that would paint the portrait in such a spectacular light, not in a way that would leave one completely speechless.

"It looks perfect." Before the battle of wits could even begin, Ocean surrendered and sulked over to the sofa and took a seat beside Max.

"What's wrong?"

"The portrait….it looks beautiful in here."

Not only was Ocean beautiful she was intriguing, Max was completely enamored. "And that's bad because—?"

"Because the only reason I came over here was to convince you to sell me *my* portrait, but seeing it now and how perfect it looks…I don't know."

"So, you came to seduce me?"

Ocean smiled and leaned back against the sofa then turned to face Max. "Yeah, some seductress I am, I couldn't even manage to keep my heels on for an hour."

"You still look great, just more *you* now, more relaxed."

In spite of herself Ocean found herself quite taken with Max. As she looked around his library lounge in addition to the Degas she noticed some other beautifully painted and carefully placed portraits. Somewhat subtly yet all at once she found herself surrounded by the likes of Frida Kahlo, Gustave

Courbet, Salvador Dali and Rembrandt. This one room in Max's townhome was better than any museum she'd visited in her entire life.

"So, Max."

"Yes, Ocean?"

"What exactly is it that you do? You've got some pretty pricy paintings hanging from your walls. How is it that you, Mr. Casual, came by such exquisite taste?"

"You're one to talk Mademoiselle." Max stood up and extended his hand to Ocean. "This sounds like the makings of dinner conversation."

Ocean switched her wine glass from her right hand to her left then with a mockingly elegant wave she placed her hand in his. "Lead the way, sir."

Back in the kitchen with both their wine glasses refreshed and two heaping bowls of deliciously aromatic bowls of paella in front of them, Ocean looked across the table and raised an eyebrow at Max. "And you cook too? I'm starting to feel like maybe I'm not the only one who had ulterior motives for this evening. I feel like maybe you want something, or you're up to *something*...I don't know."

"Really? I thought I'd been pretty obvious about my intentions. I want to get to know you. And no, I don't cook. I have however mastered the re-heat feature on my oven." With his glass raised towards Ocean and his eyes dancing across the table, Max nodded and winked. "Cheers to you, Ocean."

Comfort, casual, and rich were things that usually never went together not so far as Ocean knew; Max had completely confounded her. More confusing was how at ease she was with him and more importantly, content. One might dare say, she was having a good time. "So, what do you do Max?"

"I own a few successful companies. Rather I *owned* a few successful companies."

"Owned?"

"Yes, I started selling a few recently. I've been working so much I barely had time to live. I inherited my father's marketing and import/export business, among other things. He'd been grooming me since childhood to take over when I was old enough and when he passed away, I took over. I always knew I would take over, I just never figured it would be so soon. My father passed just before my twenty-fifth birthday. It was a hell of a birthday gift. I wake up on my twenty-fifth birthday responsible for billions of dollars and thousands of lives. It was a *lot*. Don't get me wrong, I'm thankful for everything I have and I'm extremely proud of everything I've done, I just want something different. I want something a little less than what I had and a little more than what I could ever hope for."

Max's words were like a weight coming off Ocean's chest, a weight she didn't realize she'd been carrying. To a lot of people what Max said wouldn't have made much sense but it was exactly what Ocean had been feeling most of her life. She wanted less than what she had growing up and more than what she knew. A loud sigh of relief escaped her mouth and her shoulders relaxed.

"It looks like you understand what I mean."

Ocean shut her eyes and smiled and took a breath. "I do."

CHAPTER ELEVEN

"Maxwell, love, it's good to see you. How are you feeling this evening?"

"I'm good, Amelia. Thank you for asking. You look wonderful this evening by the way, and Greg, you're as pretty as ever."

As Greg pulled out Amelia's chair for her, he looked across at Max and shook his head. "Fuck you."

"Gregory, not so loud we're in public." Amelia quickly scanned the restaurant to make sure no one had overheard Greg's *outburst.*

This monthly rendezvous for the three of them had been something Max had fought against initially. He knew Amelia, he'd known her longer than he'd known Greg and while he and Amelia had never had any kind of real falling out with one another, Max couldn't stand being around her for too long. He also resented having to get dressed up to have dinner with the two of them, it felt like some weird dog and pony show and he had no interest in trying to compete. Max didn't care how they looked and he certainly wasn't trying to impress them or anyone else. But, because his friend had asked him to, he sucked up whatever resentment he had towards starched collars and he fancied up for the evening. Despite his efforts he could see that, in Amelia's eyes, he was still underdressed and his attempt to be *presentable* was neither acknowledged or appreciated. Nevertheless, he continued to smile and be polite and say all the things he knew Amelia wanted to hear. This tactic always made the evening go quicker. "Never mind him, Amelia, you look far too lovely this evening to be stressed out over this savage."

Sitting there in his khakis and his long sleeve button up which he covered with a navy-blue sweater, and yes, this passed as Max's definition of *fancy* nowadays, looking at the three of them one might conclude that Max was on an interview or facing reprimand or in some kind of scenario where he was inferior to Amelia and Greg. The irony of it all was that despite all their airs and pretentiousness the two of them would never be on the same status level as Max. Unlike Amelia and Greg, Max was well liked, well respected, exceedingly intelligent, humble, *and* generous. He also had as much money as he had compassion, which is why there wasn't a charity on the West Coast that didn't know his name.

The one silver lining to their monthly dinners was the restaurant where they met. Once they arrived, they didn't need to study the menu and the staff were all quite familiar with them. That evening, like many before it, their usual drinks were set down in front of them before they had even thought to place their orders.

"So, Maxwell, how is retired life treating you? Gregory told me that you've just finalized the sale of another one of your holdings."

"No business talk please—that was the agreement." Not wanting the evening soured before they even received their entrees, Greg tapped his finger on the table as he quickly thought of a new subject to change the conversation to. As dearly as he loved Amelia, he considered the woman to be a shark. Her intensity and ruthlessness were part of the reason he loved her but he loved Max more and he wasn't about to let his predator of a fiancée prey on the one person he'd be willing to die for. "Amelia, did I tell you Max had a date over the weekend?"

The anticipation of a possible scandal quickly dismissed any ill feelings that may have been brewing in Amelia. "No—you didn't, but please, do tell."

Max chuckled as he nodded at Greg and took a sip of his whiskey.

Greg picked up his glass and nodded in kind before turning his gaze to a highly intrigued Amelia. "He went out with my *temp*."

"Your temp?" Amelia frowned, looking slightly disgusted as she slowly leaned back against her seat. As best she could she un-furrowed her eyebrows and tried to smile at Max. "His temp?"

Max smiled and shook his head. "She is so much more than that."

Horrified by what she was hearing Amelia placed one hand on her chest as she quickly took a sip of her Martini. "Really Gregory, you set him up with your *temp*? You couldn't think of a single person better for him than your hired help?"

"Hey, believe me, it was not my idea. The last thing I want for him is to be dating Oceana Wade."

Completely unbothered by Greg's comments, Max smiled and shut his eyes as he thought of Ocean. "She's an amazing woman. I don't know what your problem is with her. She's smart, she's attractive and she puts up with you, so she's got to have a lot of patience and strength."

With her right index finger in the air and her left hand tilting back the last of her Martini, Amelia signaled their waiter and tapped the bottom of her glass with her pinky indicating the need to refresh her drink. She turned her attention back to Max. "So, this is serious then?"

"Well, we're still getting to know each other."

"Maxwell, you can't be serious. Greg, tell him he can't be serious. She's beneath you."

Not expecting for Amelia to say what she had just said, Greg shifted awkwardly in his seat. Max on the other hand sat straight up ready to defend the honor of a woman who wasn't there.

"Amelia, that was too much," Greg, sensing the change in the atmosphere, quickly interjected before Max could respond. He was still somewhat taken aback by her statement and tried to quickly scramble and resolve the situation before it blew up, but Amelia was talking much faster than he could think that evening.

"Well she *is*, Gregory. What's wrong with stating the facts?"

Greg glanced across the table at Max who had finished his whiskey and was looking off to the side. "It's just not okay, Amelia. Yes, she's a temp but that doesn't mean she's an inferior person because of that." Much to Greg's relief the waiter brought back another round for all three of them, not just Amelia. After taking a much-needed gulp of whiskey, Greg tilted his head in the direction of Max's gaze trying to pull his friends attention back to the table. "Look, it's not because she's a temp or because she dresses like a hobo, or even because she's broke; it's because she's a Wade. She and all the women in her family are money hungry, soul-sucking succubae and I don't want her taking advantage of you. Her mother, her mother's mother and her mother before that—they've all got a reputation. They're beautiful women who go out and find these emotionally needy men and seduce them and then they bleed the poor bastards dry and move on to the next."

Generally, Max enjoyed sipping his whiskey but as he listened to Greg and tried to keep himself composed, he managed to finish off the whiskey that had just been placed in front of him in two gulps. "I know all about Ocean's mother and her grandmother and so on. She's not them. I actually met her mother when I was on business in New York six years ago. She was quite something and she was everything you say she was. Maritza Wade was stunningly beautiful even in her old age she could still rival any women on the cover of Vogue. I spoke with her briefly when I was there and *my God*, did the woman have gall. When she couldn't pick me up herself, she tried to pawn me off on her daughter, whom mind you was absent from the event but Maritza of course had pictures of her on her cell phone which she was more than happy to share with me. Maritza was sure I would find Ocean attractive and I did, so we called her. As sure as she meant it a few months ago at the art auction, she meant it six years ago back in New York; when Maritza passed me the phone all I could hear was the sound of Ocean's sweet voice telling me to *fuck off*."

Greg was completely blindsided. He'd thought he'd been keeping something from Max, protecting him from the truth and the whole time it was Max keeping secrets from him. "You met Maritza Wade? So, you and Oceana have known each other this whole time?"

The confusion on Greg's face and in his voice had amused Max to the point where all of his previous tension he had which had been induced by Amelia, had finally eased. "No. She had no idea who I was when we saw each other at the art auction. Ocean and I never actually met in New York; it really was a quick call. After she told me to fuck off, she went on to say that *her father didn't raise her to be anybody's sugar baby. She couldn't be bought and she'd never be up for sale.* Then she hung up on me. Maritza was furious. Ocean ended the call so fast I don't think I even got to tell her my name."

Disbelief still shown clearly on his face. Greg leaned back and rubbed his palms on his legs and shook his head. "I can't believe you never told me about this. And where was this? What event?"

"It was some formal event, Maritza complained about Ocean's lack of appreciation for formal wear, she complained about how Ocean's father had ruined her, how he'd taken all the dainty out of her and replaced it with crass." Anticipating more questions, comments and insults, before either Amelia or Greg could say anything Max was backing away from the table. "I appreciate you guys coming out to have dinner with me but I'm really not that hungry this evening so I'm just going to go. I hope you two enjoy the rest of your night." As he stood over the table Max looked down at the both of them to be respectful but he was really only talking to Greg. "I will say this one last thing before I go. I appreciate your concern and I'm grateful for it and I'm not crazy and I am perfectly competent to make my own decisions. I don't expect either of you to be friends with Ocean; but I do expect for you both to respect my choices. This isn't some overnight whim type of thing. I've been wanting to know this woman since the very first time she told me to fuck off, and now I have the chance, so I'm gonna take it."

PART II

KISMET

CHAPTER TWELVE

"You wanted to see me, Mr. Edwards?"

"Yes, come in and shut the door, please."

With a deep breath and a little bit of posture straightening, Ocean closed the door and readied herself to be insulted. Greg was always insulting her. "What can I do for you?"

Greg leaned back in his seat and stared at Ocean for a minute. He hated when she stood in front of him rather than taking a seat, so he'd always have to push his chair back slightly and lean backwards to avoid looking up at her and her looking down on him which in his opinion, she was nowhere near qualified to do. "Have you been talking to my clients again?"

"Well—what do you mean? I kind of *have* to talk to your clients to do my job."

"I mean, have you been handing out legal advice, again?"

Cautiously Ocean took a small step forward and placed her hands on the back of the seat Greg had wanted her to sit in. "Legal advice? No. Not that I can recall."

"You don't remember telling one of my clients last week that they'd be better off saving the money that they would spend in legal fees suing their neighbors for damages done to their property and instead submit a claim through their insurance?"

"Well—I did say that, but it wasn't legal advice, it was just my opinion. Their legal fees would be three times higher than their insurance deductible and the damages were covered so I didn't get—"

"You don't need to *get* anything. It's not your place to suggest when someone does or does not need legal representation. That's far above your pay grade."

And there was the first insult. This was a soft hit, Ocean was prepared for another. "*She* asked *me*, what *I* would do. What was I supposed to say?"

"Certainly not what you said. We lost a client because of you. You do realize my clients are the only reason you have a job? It's not rocket science. No clients equal no money, which equals no paycheck. I thought you were smart enough to at least get that. I didn't think I'd have to explain something so simple to you."

And the hits kept coming. Ocean took it all on the chin with ease. She'd decided when she came back to work for Greg that she wouldn't let him get under her skin. The way she saw it, Gregory Edwards was a bully and the only sure way to beat a bully was to never let them get the best of you. "My apologies, Mr. Edwards. Don't worry, it won't happen again. Was there anything else you wanted to discuss?"

Mildly annoyed by her calm response, Greg jerked forward and turned his attention to the computer screen in front of him and raised his hand dismissively in Ocean's direction. "No, that's all. You can go."

Oceans was quite proud of herself as she left Greg's office but her feelings of satisfaction quickly faded when she arrived back at her desk and was greeted by a very impatient Amelia.

"Finally! Where have you been? Leaving your desk unattended for this long during operational hours is completely unprofessional, I'll have you know. Who trained you?"

"Who *trained* me?" As if she were some sort of dog or something. Ocean was speechless. There was nothing she could think of saying in that moment that would have come out nicely or the least bit professional.

"I'm here to see Gregory." Instead of giving Ocean the courtesy or respect of looking her in the face as she spoke, Amelia looked down at her camel colored suede coat which she'd draped over her arm and she fussed about the collar.

"I don't see that Mr. Edwards has any appointments scheduled for this afternoon. Was he expecting you? Are you a new client?"

"A *client*? God, no. I am a lawyer, sweetheart. I don't need to hire one. I'm Gregory's fiancée, Amelia. Please, let him know that I'm waiting." Amelia checked her watch and sighed, she was visibly annoyed with Ocean for asking such ridiculous questions and wasting her precious time during her unscheduled visit.

The grin Ocean plastered across her face was so forced it appeared as if she had no lips at all. "Mr. Edwards, there's an Amelia—Amelia…" Lifting an eyebrow, Ocean looked up at Amelia who turned to the side pretending she didn't know Ocean was politely prompting her for her last name. "Your fiancée, sir. She's here in the waiting area."

After placing the phone back on the receiver Ocean stood up and brushed down her poncho sweater as she stepped around her desk. "If you'll please follow me, *Ms. Walcott*."

After leading Amelia to Greg's office, where she swept in and closed the door in Ocean's face, Ocean sighed and looked up at the ceiling, "And the hits keep coming."

"Gregory, you really should find better help. Your secretary is completely useless."

CHAPTER THIRTEEN

At a small café just a few blocks from his office, Greg sat across from Amelia confused by her unexpected visit to his office. Usually when Amelia introduced herself it was always *Amelia Elizabeth Walcott*, and she did so with a certain tone to her voice but today with Ocean, she was suddenly, *Amelia, his fiancé*. He'd seen insecure women mark their territory before, he just never realized Amelia was one of them. "So, what is it that happened that got you out your office in the middle of the work day?"

"Why does something have to have happened for me to want to come and spend time with you?" Amelia could barely take herself seriously as she responded to Greg. She giggled knowing there was no way Greg would find that believable but she decided to give herself a pat on the back anyway for at least making the attempt to stroke his ego. As her laughter faded, she let out a serious sigh and dropped her folded arms across the table. "I lost two clients today. Two! Can you believe that? Without any warning, no explanation. They just up and left."

Since he himself was sure he'd be returning to work shortly, Greg sat and sipped his expresso as he listened, he decided he'd leave the mid-day Martini drinking to Amelia. "Were they big clients?"

"*All* my clients are big clients, Gregory. You're missing my point. Somethings going on. They had no reason to leave, no complaints, no disagreements, nothing. They just up and left. Someone's poaching my clients that's what I think; but *who* and *how*? I mean, I'm a great attorney, why would they want to leave me?"

At the start of the impromptu lunch, Greg found himself feeling somewhat flattered but now that fleeting feeling of flattery had turned into cautious cynicism. Never before had Amelia come to Greg for advice about anything as far as it pertained to her job. Amelia considered corporate law far superior to criminal law and she had no problem sharing her opinions of how backward and barbaric the use of a courtroom was in this day and age. Rare was the occasion when she asked for work advice but when she did, it certainly wasn't from Greg. He knew that her *woe is me* speech was just a lure but Greg decided to bite anyway. "Did you ask them where they were taking their business? Has there been any gossip around the office?"

"No, and no. Why do I care where they're headed? They're gone. And just so you know, *my* office is not the type of office that entertains gossip. We're all far too busy for that."

Still dangling from the hook she'd dropped but also thinking of the mountain of work waiting for him back at his office, Greg decided to cut to the chase. "Is there anything I can do to help?" For a second he thought he actually saw a twinkle in Amelia's eye as she looked over at him and smiled.

"Well, and before you say no, I want you to hear me completely out." She didn't wait for Greg to affirm that he would listen she only paused for effect. "As you know, I have one of the most extensive client lists at my firm." Amelia loved bringing up her client list to everyone and anyone who would listen. What she didn't bring up however was the fact that she didn't build her extensive client list, she inherited it from her father who retired from the same firm a few years ago. "For me—losing clients, *any client*, it reflects poorly on my reputation. Although the clients I lost will do little to affect my numbers, that's irrelevant. It's the principle of it all. I don't want people to think I've lost my touch." Here it was, the big push, the bottom line, Amelia cleared her throat and made a valiant effort to soften her eyes and look *sweet*. "I was hoping you'd talk to Maxwell and convince him to sign with me. I promise no one would work harder for him and he won't have to worry about a thing."

Amelia's desire to have Max as a client, the *big* feather in her cap, was a topic of great contention for the two, but an issue that Amelia refused to let go despite them having decided a long time ago that they would not discuss Max and his business ventures since it caused so much friction between the two of them. But nevertheless, every few months Amelia would find a way to bring it up.

"You got me out of work for this?" Greg was pissed. He decided he'd missed enough of his work day trying to spend quality time with Amelia. He quickly flagged down the waitress and reached for his wallet while shaking his head in irritation. "How many times are we going to do this? He already said no, Amelia. Leave it the hell alone. Leave the man alone and stop asking me to intervene."

"Gregory, be serious for a moment, please. Think of this as business, take the emotion out of it for just a moment and try and give me one good reason why Maxwell shouldn't be my client."

"Because he doesn't want to be your client!"

Amelia anticipated resistance from Greg, but she'd hoped that by bringing him to public place in the middle of the day that it would help in keeping his temper in control. "Gregory, calm down. We're in public, don't make a spectacle."

Greg was incensed to the point where he'd accidently left enough money on the table to pay their tab ten times over. After throwing the money down he abruptly jerked at the sides of his suit jacket and fumbled around the buttons as he tried to fit them back on their proper holes. "Amelia, you need to let this go. *Do not*, under any circumstances, bring this up with Max. I mean it. Let it go."

Greg left the café agitated and fidgety. He couldn't understand why Amelia continued to pick this same fight with him again and again. It was a fight she would never win. Max would never agree to sign on as Amelia's client. He didn't even like Amelia, he only tolerated her because of Greg. Max had made himself more than clear on more than one occasion that he'd never work with Amelia or anyone at her company.

And while Max tolerated Amelia, she was walking a thin line with him. His patience had its limits and Amelia had tested them a time or two too many. Eventually Max would write her off completely and have nothing to do with her at all. Greg was infuriated, he couldn't understand why she couldn't see what she was doing. If Max walked away, Greg would have to go with him, Greg knew this and as much as he loved Amelia, in that moment he hated her, why was she trying to force him into a position where he would have to choose. For him, there wasn't a choice, it wasn't a question… it was Max. It would always be Max. Amelia was the woman he wanted to spend the rest of his life with but Max was the reason he had a life at all.

CHAPTER FOURTEEN

"So, we're really gonna do this?" Ocean held her cell phone in her hand and smiled at Max who was already dialing.

"Oh, I'm doing it already. I don't know what you're waiting for."

"This is insane."

After hitting send on his phone, Max looked up at Ocean and laughed. "I've been accused of being a little nutty."

Ocean took a breath and started dialing. "Me too."

Over the next hour the doorbell to Max's condo rang so many times the echo of the melody had Ocean feeling as if she were at some sort of amusement park. They took turns getting up to answer the door; despite the size of his home and his bank account, Max liked to do things for himself. So, that evening with no one there to answer the door for them, no staff, no *hired help*, which he really didn't have too much hired help anyway, just a cleaning lady that stopped by three times a week; Max and Ocean both got their fair share of exercise getting up and down and running back and forth until the last order came in.

Typically when people first start dating, they don't spend their holidays together. It's socially accepted that spending the holiday together indicated a certain level of seriousness that the relationship had reached and it was too soon to call what Ocean and Max had a *relationship* but here it was Thanksgiving and they were together.

They sat side by side on Max's big lush sofa in his living room. An outsider would never suspect the pair barely knew each other. The chemistry between them was undeniable and so refreshing. To the outward eye it appeared as if the two had known each other all their lives.

"I think this Thanksgiving is the best one I've ever had." Ocean looked over at Max and smiled then stared in amazement at the buffet before her. Since neither could cook but both wanted to participate in the over indulgence that was the hallmark of the holiday, instead of wasting time trying to prepare a home cooked meal, they called a total of nine restaurants and had dinner brought to them. "Should we be *civilized* and get plates or are you okay with eating everything out of the containers?"

Max looked at Ocean and winked.

"Containers it is." In her thirty plus years of life, Ocean couldn't remember a time when she'd been this excited about spending time with anyone for the holidays. Even when her father was alive, she hated the holidays, her mother would always drag them off to some formal event where everyone would be overdressed but were always underfed. This Thanksgiving with Max was a dream come true. "So, what do you wanna watch first?"

"When *Harry Met Sally*. The classic of all classics." Max kicked his feet up and grabbed a carton of Pad Tai off the coffee table. "Now, this is how everyone should spend Thanksgiving. Good food, good company, and no stress. What do you usually do on the holidays?"

Ocean looked into the box of Kung Pao Shrimp she was holding and picked at the pieces inside with her chopsticks as if she were searching for a happy memory underneath one of the spicy crustaceans, "Nothing really. Usually I just end up grabbing a pizza, a bottle of tequila, and sit and watch the parade on TV. Nothing too exciting. By the end of the evening you can usually find me in my living room dancing around to Van Morrison and Janis Joplin. Then the next day I usually get up and go to work. Pretty boring. I wasn't exactly *well liked* by too many people back in New York. I mainly kept to myself."

"Now that's a crying shame. They missed out on an amazing opportunity."

By the time *When Harry Met Sally* was over the two had barely put a dent in the mountain of takeout. After a quick tour through the rest of the town house, which had more rooms in it than Ocean thought it did, there was one room in particular that Ocean would have never expected to see there. After the tour they ended up in the library lounge. "You and Greg must be pretty close for you to let him just have a room at your house?"

"Yeah, me and Greg go way back. We pretty much grew up together."

"So, you're from Chicago then, too?"

"Yeah. We actually met by accident, Greg and I. I was fifteen, he was thirteen. When we met it was like finding the brother I never knew I lost. He is truly the very best friend a person could ever wish for."

"I'll take your word on that." Even though she felt what Max was saying was completely ridiculous, Ocean didn't want to be rude and laugh or scoff in the man's face. Instead of mocking him she slowly walked towards the end of the room and gently ran her fingers over the ivory keys of the baby grand before sitting down at the piano bench.

Max grinned and stuck his hands in his pockets as he slowly walked over to Ocean and took a seat beside her. With a small jerk of his elbow, he gently poked at her side as he exhaled deeply. "Greg's not a bad guy. He's just trying too hard to prove himself right now and he can sometimes rub people the wrong way, I know. But

he really is a standup guy. If you knew him, you'd like him, you'd really, *really* like him. I swear."
"So tell me about him."

Max's fingers, now on the ivory keys, found the melody of one of Ocean's favorite songs. "It's not really my place to tell you who he is, that's for him to do. I can tell you that you two have a lot more in common...so much more in common than you realize."

"Is that so?"

"It is. In fact, I can tell you one of those things right now...Van Morrison. Greg *loves* Van Morrison."

Ocean smiled and bumped Max on the shoulder. "That's not anything special, who doesn't love Van Morrison?" Ocean closed her eyes and swayed to the melody. It wasn't Van Morrison he was playing but it was soulful and mellow—a lot like her. As Max continued to play, she began to sing. She sang the most soulful version of *I Want to Hold Your Hand,* that Max had ever heard.

CHAPTER FIFTEEN

"On Thanksgiving Day, he dumps me. Dumps *me*! Who breaks up with someone on a holiday? I mean, how cold hearted could you be?"

Normally, she was far from being someone who liked to shop, but the Friday after Thanksgiving was the exception. She loved a good sale and she looked forward to this day each year. However, her highly anticipated Black Friday had turned into a blue and bleak day thanks to Jentri's whining. "Well, what happened? Something had to have happened. I mean, you two were all set to get married next month." Jentri's exaggerated, sigh annoyed Ocean. Not only was Jentri being mellow dramatic but she was slowing Ocean down.

"Nothing happened...not really. I mean—we were having a very calm conversation around the table over Thanksgiving. His mom and some of his family had stopped by and they all of course wanted to know how the wedding planning was going. And then, his mom— *major bitch* by the way, she makes some ridiculous comment about me needing to get *two* jobs to cover the cost of the wedding. So, I said, *I don't work, that's why I have Jeff.* Anyway, we all laughed and then at the end of the night after everyone had left he tells me, the wedding is off. He tells me, he thinks it would be a good idea for me to get my career established and he thought it would be *beneficial* for me to pour all of my energy into that instead of party planning. So, I told him, he lost his mind. I wasn't working when he met me and I certainly wasn't going to start now."

Rummaging through the clearance bin of bags at Macys, Ocean frowned as she listened to Jentri whine on about her *almost* failed marriage. "So—he didn't actually break up with you, he just called off the wedding?"

"Ocean, focus. He called off the wedding and told me to get a job! If that's not a break up what would you call it?"

"A condition." Jentri scowled at Ocean but she was too busy rummaging through the various discount purses in front of her to care what Jentri's face looked like.

"More like an ultimatum! I could understand if I had a job when we met, or I talked about wanting to work but neither was ever the case. He knew what he was getting into when he proposed so why should I have to change? I shouldn't! And I'm not going to."

"So—?"

"*So*, we got into a huge fight and he kicked me out."

Slowly Ocean stopped digging through what seemed like a bottomless box of bags and she stood up and faced Jentri. "He threw you out?"

"Yes! He threw me out. Can you believe it? What an ass, right?"

As casually as she could, Ocean crossed behind Jentri and began to pilfer though a rack of belts and accessories. "So, where will you stay?"

"With you."

"With me?"

"Of course. Where else am I gonna go? It's okay if I stay with you, isn't it?"

Despite expecting this was the direction the conversation was headed, Ocean felt a sharp pain in her gut which she quickly disguised with a smile as she turned around to face her friend. "Of course you can stay with me. We're friends, aren't we?"

"Yes, we are. And as my friend I'm hoping you could help me with one other thing. It's nothing major, I promise."

With her happy carefree shopping day officially ruined, Ocean folded her arms and eyed Jentri suspiciously. "What?"

"I need you to help move my things."

"Move your things? That's all?"

"Yeah."

"Sure. When do you have to get your stuff out by?"

"Today."

"*Today?*" Ocean stomped her foot and rolled her eyes over the impending agony. "Jentri—today? Really?"

"I know, I know, this probably is the last thing you want to be doing today but I have no choice. If I don't have my stuff out by the end of today the bastard's gonna put everything I own out on the street. Please, Ocean?"

Luckily for Jentri, Ocean was more appreciative of her friendship than Jentri was respectful of Ocean's free time. Ocean surrendered to the depressing fact that she'd be saving much more money today then she intended, she let go of the fistful of belts and gave a solemn nod to the bin of bags. "Fine, let's go. But we're stopping for breakfast first. And by the way, you're buying."

Not being able to discover the deal of the year as she intended to that morning, Ocean decided to get the most she could out of her free breakfast from her new houseguest. Knowing that breakfast would be the best part of her day, once they were seated at the restaurant and the food was brought out, Ocean did her best to make the meal last as long as she possibly could. But, after over an hour of eating and drinking, she couldn't take it anymore and had to waive the white flag.

"I feel full for you. How the hell do you eat like that? You ate enough food in that one sitting to feed ten grown men. Seriously, I got nauseous just watching you eat." Jentri cringed as she thought about the small mountain of food she'd watched Ocean shove into her mouth. They'd ordered crepes, a cheese omelet, fresh fruit, bacon, home fries, and a plate of warm croissants; Jentri had only enjoyed a Mimosa and half a croissant leaving all the rest to Ocean. "It makes no sense how you look the way you do and eat the way you eat. I swear, you're living proof that God is a man 'cause no woman would ever be so cruel as to create a woman like you. You eat what you want, you say what you want, you don't even try and look attractive and you're gorgeous. You're like a bad joke—women spend hours each day trying to look like you and you—you literally wake up like that. It's not fair, it's such bullshit."

"Thanks...I think."

After Jentri's speech on the sardonic humor of the Creator, the two women exited the restaurant and headed to Jeff's place. As soon as they entered Jeff's condo, Ocean was overwhelmed by feelings of both amazement and appall. This guy had money and by the looks of the place he didn't ever want the fact that he had money to be a question, he wanted to shove it in your face and reassure you he had it. The floors inside the condo were Italian marble, the walls Venetian plaster, in the living room an antique French settee which was obviously for show but not for sitting. There was a hand-crafted suede sofa with distressed leather trim. In the kitchen, atop the expanse of marble countertops that seemed to sparkle, there was a long envelope that had Jentri's name sprawled across the front of it.

After quickly reviewing the folded message inside, Jentri huffed and passed the letter to Ocean, Even the paper screamed *rich*—thick and soft, it let you know by holding it between your fingers that it didn't come in bulk and you wouldn't find it at your friendly neighborhood super center. This was *classy* paper. As she unfolded the letter, Ocean took a quick whiff of the arrogance that wafted off of it and turned up her nose.

Jentri-

I've taken the liberty of packing your things. Don't look for the jewelry purchased for you while we were together, I've returned all those pieces. You may hold on to the engagement ring you are so fond of since it may be the only way for you to support yourself from now on. I expect I will not see you here anymore after today because such a visit would constitute trespassing. Best of luck to you. I hope you find a man whose love for you runs as deep as his pockets.

-Jeff

"Wow." Ocean was floored.

CHAPTER SIXTEEN

"So, what do you think?"

The grimace on Max's face clearly showed how uncomfortable he was in the very expensive tailored suit. "It's nice, I like it."

Greg laughed and shook his head. "Yeah, you might wanna tell that to your face." Greg turned in the full-length mirror checking every angle making sure the suit was as perfect as it could be.

"I just never understood spending so much money on a single day. A day you're not even allowed to be comfortable." Max fiddled with the collar of his shirt then sighed in aggravation as he accepted the fact that nothing he did to the collar was going to make the suit any less *a suit* and him anymore comfortable in it. The suit itself actually fit like a glove, the real issue for Max was the fact that he had to wear it. He just wasn't a suit and tie type of guy. "I still can't believe you're doing this by the way."

Unlike Max, Greg was very pleased with the way the suits had turned out and even happier with the way he looked in his. Suit aside, it wasn't too difficult to make Greg look good, he was genetically gifted and would look good in anything. Max was no slouch, but he was also no Greg. "Doing what? The suit? It's not that expensive and anyway it's my wedding. If there was ever a time to splurge—"

"Not the suit. The wedding."

Greg rolled his eyes as he unbuttoned his tux and slowly began to remove the jacket. "Jesus Christ, would you give it a rest?" He decided not to argue with Max in that moment and stomped his way into the dressing room. Alone in the dressing room of the shop, Greg stepped out of the tux and yanked on his pants and mumbled angrily to himself.

"What's that *Gregory?* I can't hear you sweetheart, you'll have to speak up." It wasn't Max's intent to piss Greg off but he also had no intentions on lying to him either. Whenever the conversation steered towards Greg's impending nuptials he made it quite clear that he thought his friend was making a bad decision. Even in light of his displeasure, he was still the *best man*. No matter who the bride was, Max had always known where he'd stand on Greg's wedding day. The fact that he thought Amelia was the wrong woman would never stop him from being the best man.

Max's impersonation of Amelia was dead on. Trying as hard as she could to contain his laughter Greg stepped out of the dressing room and shoved Max on the shoulder. "Keep it up wise guy. You're one to talk anyway, how are things going with you and Oceana?"

"Great. We spent Thanksgiving together. We ordered in, she's as lousy a cook as I am apparently. We watched movies and she sang—did you know she could sing? I mean she can *really* sing. We had a great time. She's—"

"A Wade. So be careful."

As he unbuttoned his shirt and headed towards the dressing room, Max smiled to himself. "She's not who you think she is. Also, just so you know, when it comes to her I don't want to be careful, I wanna be fearless."

"Okay, *Captain Fearless*, just don't let her play you and turn you into *Captain Careless.*" Out of the dressing room and back into his jeans Max was visibly happier which amused Greg. "It's not gonna kill you to wear a nice suit for a couple of hours for one day."

"It might." Outside the store the two men seemed to be on two separate pages. Where Greg was going left, Max was heading right. "Where the hell are you going? The sub shop is this way."

"Just one more stop. I promise."

"More wedding shit?" As Max turned his head in the direction he wished they were headed, he sighed then dropped his head as he followed behind Greg to the left of the tux shop.

"You're so freaken dramatic. You're not gonna starve if we push lunch back thirty minutes. You eat enough in one sitting to cover you for the entire day anyway. I know you ate breakfast so you're good for a while, relax."

The bakery where the two headed was less than a fifteen-minute walk from the tuxedo shop. The bakery owner, who wasn't in, had been expecting Greg that morning and before stepping out that afternoon she had left his bill up front with her assistant who promptly called out the total for his order.

"Five thousand dollars! For a cake? Greg, you've got to be kidding me? Who spends five grand on a cake?"

"It's two cakes actually. Her cake and my cake. It's actually not a bad price for the both of them and mine is carrot cake. You love carrot cake."

Max stared at the receipt that he'd snatched from Greg. "I've yet to taste a carrot cake that I'd be willing to waste hundreds on. Which by the way brings me to another question I had, why are you paying for the cake? Shouldn't she be paying for the cake? What happened to the *Father of the Bride* footing the bill? Isn't that tradition? Besides I'm sure it wasn't *your* idea to have a groom's cake. What else are you paying for?"

"Don't worry about it. All you have to do is show up and have a good time, let me worry about everything else. Oh, and your speech, Amelia wanted me to remind you, don't forget to write your speech."

As they back tracked down the sidewalk making their way to the sub shop, Max was silent and Greg was getting agitated. "What? What is it now? You're still upset about the cake? Don't eat the damn thing if it makes you that upset."

"It's not the cake, well—not just the cake. It's the cake, the tux, the dinner menu, the hall, the limo it's everything. Hell, it's you. Look at you. I mean, Christ, it's Saturday, you're hanging with your best man, your best friend and you're dressed like you're going to a God damn christening. And what's with the grooming? The eyebrows and the hair—why can't you just throw on a pair of jeans and a sweatshirt in the morning and be fine with that? I promise I won't judge you for looking like you spent less than five hundred dollars on an outfit."

Greg paused and turned to Max and winked. "If I didn't know any better, I'd think you were jealous."

"It's a good thing you know better, then."

Greg was as exciting when it came to food choices as he was in his choice of clothing. Where Max ordered steak and cheese with sautéed peppers and onions and a large Dr. Pepper, Greg ordered a tuna sandwich on white bread with a slice of tomato and a Pellegrino to wash it down.

"Really? You come to the sub shop and get a tuna sandwich on white bread? Who are you?"

Greg threw his hands up in surrender and laughed as he opened his Pellegrino. "Hey, not everybody can eat like shit and look like you. You're a genetic freak."

Trying to sustain the levity in the conversation but still being direct and a tad more serious Max sat back and chewed the massive bite he'd taken from his sandwich then he slowly washed it down with a sip of soda. "You know, when we first met, you were so different."

"You mean poor?"

"I mean magnetic. You had to have been one of the most interesting people I'd ever met. You were by far the one with the most heart. I never thought you'd end up becoming this— this— whatever *this* creature is, you've become."

Greg wiped his mouth and threw down his napkin. "Creature? You act like me getting married is the worst thing I could do in life."

"Not getting married...*who* you're marrying."

"For God's sake, what the hell is wrong with Amelia?"

With his mouth partially full from the bite he'd just taken Max quickly looked up at Greg and shook his head and grinned. "Why are you marrying her? You barely know her."

"What do you mean, I barely know her? We've been dating for years. Hell, we *live* together. I see her practically every day."

With the last bit of his sandwich finished Max sighed with relief. "Did you know her favorite flowers were orchids? Or that her favorite color is white? Weird, I know, but I found that one out back in grade school when we were assigned to use our favorite color for some assignment and well, Amelia's favorite color was white. And, do you know why her favorite color is white? I'll tell you why. Because diamonds are white and she loves diamonds, she said so herself. Even in grade school she was a prima donna. Let's see, what else? She thinks salvation can be bought and justice should always be for sale. She thinks poverty is contagious so she won't let poor people touch her, let alone near her, and she thinks she can manipulate her way out of any uncomfortable situation. Oh, and did I ever tell you about the time she tried to seduce my father?"

He hadn't been aware of most of what Max had said but he was completely shocked by the final statement. "Get the fuck outta here. She did not."

"Oh yes, she did. It was the year after you and I met. Amelia and I were sixteen so you were fourteen. Well, anyway, she'd been hanging around my place a lot offering to help with this and that. I come home one day and she's got her skirt rolled up and her shirt half way unbuttoned and she's leaning over the counter talking to my dad telling him in this real soft baby talk kind of voice how much she'd been wanting this diamond tennis bracelet. Before my dad could answer I walked in the room and took out my wallet and threw a couple of twenties at her. So, she shoots me this dirty look and she gets all pissed off and asks what I did that for. So I told her she was doing it wrong, *pros* always get their money up front."

"You didn't?"

Nodding as he sipped his drink, Max smiled as he remembered how angry Amelia was with him that day. "I most certainly did. She didn't talk to me for a long time after that."

"Why didn't you ever tell me this?"

"I promised her father I wouldn't say anything to anyone about it. After Amelia went home crying, her dad stopped by my place to see what happened and you know what the funny thing is? When I told him what happened, he didn't seem that surprised by Amelia's behavior. Her father's a real son of a bitch though, major con artist. I guess it shouldn't have surprised him finding out what a vicious little pretender his daughter was turning out to be. I used to think, actually— I still do think, she made her daddy real proud of her that day."

CHAPTER SEVENTEEN

By Sunday evening Greg was exhausted from his holiday weekend. Throughout the course of his four-day weekend he had only actually spent one day with Amelia, Thanksgiving Day, and to him that day felt like the longest one of all.

Greg had driven to Amelia's parent's house late afternoon on Thanksgiving Day. He wanted to arrive as close to the scheduled dinner hour as possible but still early enough to offer some last-minute assistance. Greg hated going to Amelia's parents' house. The Walcott family home was gorgeous, it sat on two acres of land just outside the city and was surrounded by nature. The place was picturesque, it was the exact image one would think of when they thought about getting away someplace in search of peace and tranquility. For Greg, visits to the Walcotts' gave him heartburn. On his last visit he'd been so tense and had been grinding his teeth so hard he'd fractured a tooth in the back of his mouth.

Despite his dislike for being around them, Greg admired the Walcotts. They were an attractive family, very successful, and he was honored to be considered part of their circle. The only problem was, was that the Walcotts had a habit of making Greg feel like he was *less than* whenever he spent time with them, and Thanksgiving was no exception. The only one to show any gratitude that day around the Walcott table was Greg himself, and it was appreciation for the dinner's end and being able to take his leave. Amelia had honored Greg's request not to discuss Max's business dealings any further, or so he thought, and Greg was appreciative but what he hadn't expected was for his manipulative minx of a fiancée to sic her dad on him, which is exactly what she did. As soon as he made his escape that evening and was in the comfort and quiet of his vehicle he immediately made a quick reminder note in his phone to schedule himself a dental appointment.

Greg hadn't seen Amelia since Thanksgiving but that didn't stop her from running him ragged every day since. It seemed as if every hour for the past two days he'd get a text from Amelia telling him to *pick up this for the wedding, pay for this for the wedding, sign this for the wedding, register this for the wedding*. In the past two days Greg felt sure he'd done more work for this wedding then most grooms did in the entirety of their engagement. At nine o'clock Sunday evening he was tired and a little resentful as he sat drinking a glass of Scotch on his living room sofa when Amelia finally decided to return home.

"Gregory, love, why are you sitting in the dark?" Amelia sashayed around the living room turning on the lights and pretending not to notice Greg's sour mood, much in the same way she'd pretended not to hear any part of the cringe worthy conversation her father had with him on her behalf just a few days prior.

"Glad to see you decided to return home." Greg turned his eyes from the nothingness he was staring into and looked at Amelia. When their eyes met he felt a twinge of surprise because he realized he wasn't glad she was home, he didn't really care at all.

"Honestly Gregory, I think we both needed a breather after how rude you were to my father at Thanksgiving. I mean *really*, telling him to mind his own business. What kind of thing is that to say to the man whose daughter you're about to marry? Speaking of, did you get everything on the list I gave you?"

"Yeah, I got it, all ten thousand dollars of it." When Amelia first got back to their condo Greg wasn't sure what he was feeling but he knew now. He was angry. As he made his way from the sofa to the bar area off the kitchen, he laughed to himself and shook his head. "You—you and your father are quite the pair. That entire dinner was nothing but a tactical assault on my friendship with Max and the two of you trying to find ways to exploit it." The Scotch in his glass had become somewhat of a liquid sedative for the night and he sighed as he sipped. "Since you insist on pushing the issue I'll just come right out with it. Max doesn't like you. He doesn't like you *or* your father. He tolerates you because of me. He's been trying for months— trying to be friendly with you but clearly you are just hellbent on solidifying all the negative feelings he's had about you since the two of you were teenagers."

Amelia wasn't at all shocked by the things Greg was saying. What did shock her was his gall to say it. How dare he try and call her out when she was quite comfortable pretending to be oblivious. "I think you've had enough to drink tonight Gregory. Put the Scotch down."

"I'll decide when I've had enough, thank you. What's wrong? You don't like hearing the truth?"

Amelia's obvious denial of Max's dislike of her was an act she worked hard at maintaining. So what if he didn't like her? Not many people did, but she knew that, she'd just decided that everyone else was either jealous of her or threatened by her and she pitied them. Max, on the other hand, was a horse of a different color. He wasn't jealous, he was smart and he wasn't threatened by her, not in the slightest. And to Amelia, he was the Holy Grail. In all the years she'd known Max she'd attempted to get close to him from every possible angle she could and she crashed and burned on every front. She'd tried flattery, bargaining, seduction, groveling and even bribery. Greg was her Hail Mary. Since she was a child she'd been obsessed with Max's family fortune and decided that their life was one that she deserved. Unfortunately, Max was an only child with no interest in her, so if she couldn't make him fall in love with her, she decided to manipulate his love for someone else, and Greg just happened to be that someone.

"Look, I know sometimes I can be a bit pushy and headstrong but it's only because I'm passionate about what I do." Mustering up all the pout and seductiveness she could manage Amelia crept up behind Greg and wrapped her arms around him and laid her face against his back. "And I know I'm not Maxwell's favorite person but I was hoping with the wedding and everything that he and I could get a little bit closer. Not just because I want him as a client but because of you. I love you, and you and I are about to make a promise to spend the rest of our lives together and Maxwell is a part of your life so that means he's a part of mine as well. I don't ever want you to feel like you have to choose between me and Maxwell. I would never put you in that position."

Somehow, Amelia said just the thing Greg needed to hear and he put the Scotch down. He wasn't pissed off anymore but he did have a lot of pent up frustration which he began to eagerly release on Amelia. Generally, Amelia liked it a little rough but she always wanted to look good while going at it, tonight Greg had no patience or respect for the ceremonial seductive undressing she liked to do and he tore open the back of her soft pink silk dress and yanked the front down. Half-naked would do for tonight and so would the end table next to the bar cart. With a fist full of her blonde hair and her body doubled over end table Greg leaned down and wrapped his free hand around her waist and pulled her head back and plunged himself into her as deeply as he could and when she gasped, he did it again. Over and over until sweat began to blind his eye and his legs began to shake.

CHAPTER EIGHTEEN

"That play was amazing. The actors, the songs—it was so amazing." Ocean was positively exuberant as she walked into Max's town house with him that Sunday evening.

Ocean had spent the entire day with Max and not even noticed it. Since Jentri had moved in with her which was only two days ago, although it felt like a lifetime ago, Ocean was feeling a desperate need for space from her bestie. She and Max had planned the night before to meet each other for breakfast at a diner not too far from Ocean's place. They'd spent so much time talking after breakfast they didn't have time to say goodbye, it didn't fit the flow of the conversation, so neither said it; they just kept talking.

After they left the diner, they chatted and laughed as they wandered around the area for a while. To see them together one might have thought they were recently engaged, or newlyweds even. They gave off strong *high school sweetheart* vibes. They looked comfortable with each other, as if they were one another's favorite woolen sweater and matching scarf.

Eventually, actually not too far into their walk they stumbled into some local shops where Max bought her some *real* novels. Max had a thing for psychological dramas; and Ocean, she got him concert tickets, which came after she'd given him a very brief yet intense lesson in music.

It was there, in the middle of the kitschy catch all store after Max had selected Ocean's *must reads*, where he mentioned he didn't particularly care for British artists, and thus began their light-hearted debate about American soul versus British soul. At Ocean's insistence Max listened to various British artists he'd never heard of before. Finding his response inadequate and the store's variety insufficient, Ocean began Googling. It only took a minute for her to discover that her favorite Brit of all time was on U.S. soil and singing live in L.A. in three weeks. Luckily for her she'd been outbid on a portrait some months ago and out maneuvered out of her day of sale shopping on Black Friday. All that involuntary saving had put her in a place where she had some extra money to spend and so she did. She purchased the best tickets she could find for her and Max to see Ed Sheeran in concert the following month.

After book buying and concert ticket purchasing, it was late afternoon and with breakfast so far behind them it only made sense that they sat and ate lunch together; and as it just so happened the restaurant where they decided to eat was right next door to a tiny little theatre, which was putting on a stage play that evening...how could they not go?

"The woman who played the lead, what a freaken voice. It was so—so—"

Max looked up from the container of Chinese food he was opening and smiled. "Soulful?"

Ocean tried not to smile but her efforts were useless. "Aren't you the witty one." With her trusty cellphone in hand Ocean jumped on the counter next to Max and searched YouTube for the best of the Brits, what she really wanted to search was *songs to make Max eat his words*. And she started with the mother of melancholy, Adele. "Now you can't tell me that Adele does not have soul. I mean seriously, listen to that."

Max nodded to the music and shoveled pieces of sautéed broccoli into his mouth as he listened. When the track ended he plopped the container down on the counter behind him then grabbed Ocean by the hand. "I'll see your Adele and I'll raise you some John Legend. Off to the library we go, Mademoiselle."

Back in what so far had become Ocean's favorite room in the entire townhome Max turned on his entertainment system so that he could match the sounds of John's pleading voice against Adele's achy alto.

"I hate to break your heart friend, especially since you were just starting to grow on me, but John doesn't stand a chance." Right before she was able to put on her best smug, indignant grin Ocean's ears caught the melody of the song Max had selected and unfortunately for her, he had chosen the one John Legend song she couldn't help but sway to.

Very pleased with himself Max stood back for a minute with his back leaned against the wall and he watched Ocean sway from side to side. After a brief moment of watching he decided to join in and he extended his hand to her as he slowly made his way to the center of the room.

"This doesn't mean you win." Ocean looked up at Max but he just smiled down at her and kept dancing. It could have been the music or it could have been the perfectness of the day; or it could have been the way Max was looking down at her. More than likely, it was everything. It was all of it, and as the intensity in John's voice grew, when the song had fully reached its crescendo, Ocean's fingers were pressed so firmly into Max's back that her nails were cherry red and at some point, the space between them had vanished and they had slowly melted into each other much like the way snow melts into the ground on a clear warm day in winter—subtle and slow yet rapid and steamy.

"Are you okay?" Nose to nose and still dancing to the song that was no longer on, Max looked down at Ocean and inhaled deeply.

The soft raspy base of Max's voice near her ear made Ocean press her fingers even harder, so much that they began to go numb. "Yeah, I'm okay. Why?"

"You were holding your breath for quite a while."

"I was?"

"You were." Max shut his eyes and smiled. He could feel the tension in Ocean's fingertips begin to release and her breast gently push against his chest as she took several deep breaths. After a few seconds of silence, the song started all over again and then all at once Ocean's hands were at either side of his neck and her upper lip was sandwiched between his bottom lip and his tongue, and then suddenly her thighs were wrapped around his waist.

She'd managed to get her breathing right again but her head was spinning as if she were still holding her breath, she could only imagine this is what John Legend must have been referring to when he sang *So High*.

On the cushiony sofa in her favorite room which belonged to the man who was quickly becoming her favorite person, Ocean sat completely naked—nothing but her luscious locks waterfalling down her back and Max's hands at her waist.

Never in her entire life had Ocean had sex like this. Hands down this was absolutely the best sex she'd ever had and she didn't want it to stop. The repeated crescendo of the song only added to the impassioned ride she was giving Max.

Between the throbbing, the panting and the biting it was unclear how many times John Legend sang his heart out for them that night. At some point during the chorus of the song, or it could have been in the beginning of the song, or the end—neither would have been able to say honestly, but somewhere during John's serenade and Ocean's final ride of the night, when she couldn't command her spine to wave anymore, with her head buried deeply in Max's neck and his arms wrapped firmly around her body Ocean bit her bottom lip and moaned as Max slowly and powerfully lunged into her from below. The event was so exhausting and so passionate it literally brought a tear to her eye.

CHAPTER NINETEEN

"Jentri, what is it? I can't talk right now, I'm at work." Crouched down as low to her desk as she could possibly get, Ocean did her best to be as polite and as patient as she possibly could to her new houseguest as she tried to hurry her off the phone.

"Ocean!"

The sound of Greg's irritated voice coming though the speaker on her phone made her think perhaps her voice was not as hushed as she hoped it was. "Yes, Mr. Edwards?"

"I'd like to see you in my office, please."

He said, *please*, maybe he hadn't heard her, maybe, just maybe he was drunk and he'd forgotten how awful he was being to her that morning. Granted she had come in late that morning but over the past several months she'd been working for Greg not only had she outlasted every temp before her but she showed up every day on time and with a smile and despite her tardiness today, she was still smiling from ear to ear.

"What can I do for you Mr. Edwards?"

Still highly annoyed that she'd arrived to work an entire *twenty-minutes* late, but not wanting the conversation to end in an explosive confrontation, Greg decided to table his annoyance for the time being. "Please, have a seat. First things first, the Stewart case. What exactly did you tell Ms. Stewart?"

Ocean was visibly confused and her scrunched up nose and perplexed stare were not just for effect. She knew Ms. Stewart but she had no idea what Greg was referring to. "I don't know. What did I say?"

"Did you tell her—hhmm, how did she phrase it? You told her she was going to sue her way straight into destitution."

Ocean let out a slight huff then casually put her left arm up on the chair's arm rest and she rested her chin on her hand and tried to hide her grin. "Oh, that. Yeah, I did say that but it slipped out, I didn't actually mean to say it and for what it's worth I was off the clock. We bumped into each other one day at the coffee shop down town and she told me she was bringing in another case and well—I don't know, maybe I did mean to say it, I don't feel like I meant to, but either way it was the truth. Honestly, I don't even know how she affords your legal fees at this point."

Greg knew Ocean was right. Ms. Stewart was bringing Greg a new case every ninety days. The woman was literally trying to sue her way to happiness and sure she was losing money on the excessive amount of law suits she filed, but Greg was winning all her cases for her and earning a great deal of money in doing so. The fact that Ocean carelessly tossed around statements that could cost him thousands of dollars made absolutely no sense to him. Not only was it nonsensical it was infuriating.

"We've been here before Oceana. But, just for clarities sake let's go through this one more time. *I'm* an attorney, people pay me to win cases for them and I do, I win cases for them. Your job is to help me win those cases so I can earn money to pay you." Greg put up his hand halting the interference he could see coming his way from Ocean. "If I lose clients, I lose money which means, *you* don't get paid. Furthermore, it's not your business how Ms. Stewart wants to spend her money. She earned it."

"Inherited it."

"Excuse me?" Greg was not one to be easily caught off guard but Ocean had done just that.

Ocean shrugged and shook her head. "Nothing."

"No, tell me what you said."

"She didn't earn her money. She inherited her money."

Greg was both shocked and intrigued. He wasn't quite sure how to broach the subject with Ocean, or at least bring it up in a way that would keep senior partner Leland Collins away from his office but much to his surprise Ocean blew the hinges off the door for him. "So, you have an issue with the way she earned her money?"

Ocean sighed in frustration. "She didn't earn it!" Her words had come out much blunter and biting than she had intended. "A man died. A man who worked hard his entire life died and left his millions to a woman he met at the end of his life and didn't get a chance to truly know and now she's just wasting it. All of it. Everything he worked for. She's just—she didn't—a man died, she inherited the money. She didn't work for it."

Greg leaned back in his chair and smiled at Ocean, not a grin but an actual smile. It was the first time she'd ever seen the man smile since she started working for him. The smile suited him, but while she found it to be an attractive added feature to his face, she also found it to be severely unnerving since she wasn't really sure what it meant or why he was doing it.

"So you're telling me that *you*, of all people, you, *Oceana Veritas Wade* don't think that she's *earned* the money she has and doesn't—rather *shouldn't* be able to spend it however she wants? What a paradox." Not only was Greg smiling but now he was laughing at her, and right in her face.

It was clear now what the smile meant and now that its meaning was clear Ocean decided she didn't care for it, and the laughter, the metaphorical twist of the knife, his callous laughter sent sharp shooting pains through her abdomen.

"What's so funny? You have something you want to say to me, Mr. Edwards?"

"My apologies Oceana, I didn't mean to laugh but you have to admit it is just a little funny. I mean, talk about ironic, right? *You* as a Wade woman have a problem with how she *earned* her money."

"Yeah—I don't see the irony and I don't appreciate the laughter. I'm not a joke, Mr. Edwards. I'm not here for your amusement or for you to mock."

"No, no please—wait, don't leave. Seriously, I didn't mean to laugh like that." As Ocean sat back down in her seat Greg watched her carefully and quietly settled back in while he composed himself. "What I meant to say was, I think it's ironic that you have a problem with Ms. Stewart and how she earned or did not earn her money considering how the women in your family have made their millions. I wasn't trying to mock you or anything, I mean its common knowledge, the women in your family are notorious black widows. Whether you like it or not you've got a reputation and its one very similar to the women whose lifestyle you're sticking your nose up at."

The sobering realization that Greg knew more about her than she wanted anyone on the West Coast to know made her feel exposed. It was as if Greg just stripped her naked and dropped her off at the entrance of Central Park West. She was quickly flooded with memories—visions of fingers pointing at her, sideways glances, women snickering; she knew what they were saying, it was just as Greg said, her mother had a reputation... but that was in New York! Never in her wildest dreams would she have thought that her mother's lifestyle, her predatory ways would have been legendary, certainly not enough to be talked about from coast to coast. Clearly Ocean hadn't given her mother enough credit.

"I am *not* my mother, Mr. Edwards." She wasn't twelve anymore, Ocean rolled her shoulders back and lifted her head and stared Greg right in the eye. "I am the product of a pragmatic decision my mother made a long time ago but make no mistake, I am my *father's* daughter. Maritza Giselle Wade was a woman in a class of her own and believe me, Mr. Edwards, I did not and do not subscribe to her school of thought. Every dime that women *wasted* was *my father's* blood, sweat, and tears. Years of hard work squandered on frilly dresses, silly hats and uncomfortable shoes. So, yes, I take offense to Ms. Stewart and how she *manages* her finances."

The top of Greg's eye lids all of a sudden appeared heavy and partly covered his bright baby blues in a way that would have been seductive had not everything about his person come off so menacing. "I'd be more apt to believe your little song and dance about how unlike Maritza you are if you weren't dating one of the wealthiest men on the West Coast."

"Max?" It was like she was on a friggin' tilt-a-whirl, Ocean was definitely not expecting Greg to say that. She didn't realize it was something he *could* say. "Max is the wealthiest man on the West Coast? According to who?"

"What do you mean, according to who? According to everyone. You're not going to convince me you didn't know he has money. I heard you Wade women were as scheming and duplicitous as you are strikingly beautiful but you not knowing Max is loaded—there's no amount of lash batting from you that's going to convince me you didn't know that."

Ocean's shoulders slowly sagged and she rubbed at her chin as if she'd just received a massive upper cut. "I mean—I know he's got money, I've been to his town house and the place is amazing. It's obvious he has money. I just didn't know he had *that* kind of money."

"Sure, you didn't." Greg sighed and leaned back in his seat. "You know his family already thinks he's nuts, and him gallivanting around with you only validates those accusation. Whatever you're planning, whatever it is you think you're gonna get outta him, I promise you, you won't."

"I—AM *NOT* MY MOTHER! I would never ever dream of trying to seduce Max for his money." Ocean could hear herself; she could hear the horror in her own voice and yet, even she wasn't convinced. She was her mother's child after all. Without any effort she ran right into the lifestyle she'd moved away from. It was as if fate were laughing at her now, like her path in life was already laid out no matter which road she chose. It was like everything was predetermined. It was kismet.

PART THREE

ASYSTOLE

CHAPTER TWENTY

After Ocean's *talk* with Greg on Monday she was left feeling a bit out of sorts. Where she was once certain of herself now she didn't know what to think or how to feel. She despised her mother and never wanted to be anything like her but had recently been presented with evidence that showed she was more like her mother then she realized; so, what did that say about her? Then there was Max. She liked Max, she really, *really* liked Max but now she also resented him. She resented him for making her fall for him and involuntarily be part of the cause of her self-loathing. Then there was Greg, she couldn't stand Greg, but she kind of admired him, too. He had called her out in defense of his friend which she found to be very honorable; especially coming from Greg, who she considered severely lacking in moral integrity. Lastly there was Jentri. Ocean loved Jentri but Jentri was getting on her nerves and as hard as she tried Ocean couldn't shake her desire for Jentri to just go away.

"I'm home." Jentri's voice was melodic and light-hearted Thursday evening when she entered Ocean's apartment. "Ocean, come out of your cave. I've got a surprise for you."

As Ocean reluctantly made her way from her bedroom to the kitchen, she silently braced herself for whatever surprise Jentri had in store for her. Ocean hated surprises.

"Ta-dah!" Jentri smiled as she threw open her arms towards the large quantity of food she had placed along the counter.

Ocean's eyes bulged as she took in the various amount of fried, sautéed and butter laden treats on her countertop. Everything she wasn't allowed to eat as a kid, everything Jentri wouldn't eat as an adult. Ocean's mood lifted slightly at the sight of it all. "Am I dying? Is this my last meal? 'Cause if it is, let me tell you, you did good kid." Ocean chuckled as she inhaled deeply and made her way to the counter to take a closer look. "But really, what's all this for?"

"Well—I know you've been a bit down this week and I don't know why, I hope it's not because of me. It's not, is it?"

Ocean glanced at Jentri over her shoulder and grinned. "No, it's not you."

"Good. Anyway, so you've been a bit down and I know you're not the party type so I thought about what would be the best way to cheer you up and I thought about how much you like food, and I figured after everything you've done for me, you know helping me move, taking me in, not charging me rent. I figured the least I could do was stop calorie counting and whining about my situation and pick up some of your favorite foods and sit and eat my feelings with you. *And* just in case we can't shove them down far enough with the carbs,

I've got a bottle of tequila we can drown the bitches in."

Eager to start this impromptu girl's night off right, Ocean poured them each a double shot of Don Julio. "Cheers to fate...that twisted, malicious, sadistic, conniving bitch!"

Curious, Jentri clanked her glass with Ocean's. She was hoping Ocean was being honest and she wasn't the reason behind her foul mood and although she wasn't completely certain she was more at ease about it after Ocean's toast. "So, you wanna talk about it?"

"Talk about what?"

Jentri watched as Ocean started portioning out multiple items of food from the large assortment of items on the counter. With her empty glass pressed softly against her lips and with her right finger rolling around the top of the counter top, Jentri quietly hummed to herself. "*What* indeed."

She'd always been squeamish about discussing romantic interest with anyone, Ocean had no intention on discussing her newfound romance with Jentri that evening and maybe it was the Don Julio, which was now half gone, or perhaps it was the cannoli, or maybe the mountain of buffalo wings she'd eaten that made Ocean put her brain on snooze and let the big steel walls she'd built around herself to slowly start sliding down. More than likely it was the need to have an honest moment with the only true friend she'd ever had.

"Okay, so first off, your boss is a total asshat for interfering in your personal business. I mean sure, he's friends with the guy but that doesn't give him the right to tell you what to do on your personal time. Maybe he's jealous. Maybe he wants you for himself."

The accusation from Jentri sent Ocean into a fit of laugher. "Greg, interested in me? Yeah, right. The man treats me like I'm the second coming of Typhoid Mary or something. But, thanks for the laugh."

Jentri chuckled and shrugged her shoulders. "Okay, so maybe he's not into you, maybe—*maybe* he's secretly in love with Max himself."

"No—Well, I think he does love Max, just not in *that* way. Besides, he's engaged."

Jentri rolled her eyes and finished the last of the tequila in her glass. "Engaged does not equal *not* gay. So what, you're just gonna stop seeing this guy—this guy who you're *really* in to all because your boss doesn't like it and he thinks you're some sort of gold digger? Clearly the man doesn't know you at all. *Gold digger* couldn't be farther from the truth."

Ocean sighed and lowered her head. "Actually Jentri, he has a valid reason to be concerned."

Watching Ocean's shoulders fall in an obvious submissive manner puzzled and concerned Jentri. "What valid reason, Ocean? You're the most basic, essential, frugal—and I don't mean this as an insult by the way, I'm just saying—you're pretty Plain Jane. You've got this Grace Kelly kind of beauty mixed with this sort of hippie; *I don't give a shit* Janis Joplin kind of vibe. And I love that about you. I love that you're pretty without trying *and I hate that you're pretty without trying.*" Jentri tossed a pillow at Ocean's head and laughed. "But of all the names I could call you, *gold digger* definitely would not be one of them. Besides, even if you were, you'd probably use all the money doing something crazy like trying to liberate all the animals from Sea World."

"Well they should be free, those animals are much too smart and too precious to be stuck behind cages, it's not right." She'd been on the fence about how far into the truth she was willing to travel this evening but she finally made up her mind. "So, here's the thing, Jentri." Ocean lifted her head to look her friend in the face as she spoke, "I come from a long line of career Femme Fatales. Beautiful women who marry rich, bear a beautiful child and then inherit all their husbands' wealth—squander their ill gained fortune then—rinse and repeat. That's my life. I grew up on Manhattan's Upper West Side, my mother was the woman that other women whispered about and hid their husbands from."
"I'm gonna need another drink." Jentri grabbed the bottle of Don Julio and quickly poured some into both

their glasses. "So, your dad was loaded? You said, the women in your family marry rich men, so that means your dad was loaded, right?"

"My father was very successful, yes."

Suddenly hit with a great gust of energy Jentri got up and stared pacing the length of the couch, deeply in thought trying to reconcile the sudden onslaught of information. "So, your dad didn't leave you anything? They never leave the kids anything?"

Ocean sighed. "He left me the one thing he knew I'd want, his original Degas portrait."

"An original Degas? Okay, so where is it?"

Ocean couldn't help but smile as she thought about the tiny little dancer portrait in question. "They sold it... the bank. When my mother pissed away every last dime my father had left her, she started buying things on credit and right before she died all the bills came due. The bank came in and took everything and put it up for auction to pay her debts. I personally think she died on purpose. Maritza Giselle Wade would rather be dead then destitute."

"But they can't do that. That's *your* portrait. Your father left it to you." Jentri plopped down on the sofa annoyed by the revelation of the auctioned off art.

"Well it's not mine now, it's Max's. That's how we met. I saved every dime I had to try and buy the portrait back, but Max outbid me."

"Aww, that's so sweet. You two fell in love over art, aw how cute." Jentri leaned on Ocean's shoulder and gave her a playful poke in the side.

Ocean quickly redirected the conversation off the mushy road it was heading down and began to clear the mess off the coffee table. "It's not love. I like him but...I don't know."

"Ocean, don't be such a snob." Jentri quickly picked up the plates Ocean left behind and trotted after her into the kitchen. "So what he's got money? You can't seriously hold that against him. Stop being so self-righteous, it's not attractive. I get it, you don't like being compared to your mother, that's fine, but your gonna run away from a perfectly good guy because of money you have no interest in, and more importantly haven't been offered; *and* probably wouldn't take even if it were offered. You are not your mother, Ocean."

Ocean turned towards Jentri and leaned her hip against the counter as she allowed Jentri's words to linger in the air. "I know but—No, you're right. I'm not my mother."

CHAPTER TWENTY-ONE

After a night of truthful conversation and tequila shots, come Friday Ocean had found her conviction again. During the day the office was too busy for her to be bothered with Greg and mulling over what he might be thinking, or what he might have said to Max about her. In addition to the nonstop calls and walk in clients that kept her away from Greg, senior partner Leland Collins had popped in to check on things and *chat* with Greg. Ocean loved it when Mr. Collins showed up unexpectedly, he was always so kind to her but what she liked the most about his visits were how they always had a way of souring Greg's day and led him to keep his distance from everyone by spending the rest of the day uncommunicative and behind his closed office door. Ocean *loved* it.

Friday flew by and before she knew it she was back at Max's town house sitting across from him in the living room.

"Penny for your thoughts." Max could clearly see something was on Ocean's mind this evening. Due to various appointments and other business-related matters that needed his attention this week, the two of them hadn't had much time to talk. When Friday finally arrived and he was free from all of his other obligations, Ocean was the first person he called. In an effort to make up for lost time he asked her to spend the entire weekend with him.

Despite how naturally relaxed the two were with each other, tonight Ocean was nervous. "I wanna tell you something but I'm not sure how you're gonna feel about it and if you want me to go after I tell you, I'll understand."

Max frowned and scooted closer to Ocean. "I doubt it, but shoot."

Ocean took a breath and tried to shake off the nerves. "Okay, so here it goes. My mom… my mom was a gold digger—and her mom was a gold-digger and so on and so on. I come from a long line of gold diggers." Ocean paused and let out a long breath of air before peaking at Max, who appeared very tentative but unalarmed. "Anyway, it was brought to my attention that you are more successful than I thought you were, and you have a great deal more money than I thought you had—not that I was thinking about your money; but anyway, I could see how it might look, someone like me being with someone like you, but I swear, I'm not my mother."

Max smiled and let out a slight chuckle. "Is that all? I know who your mother is, Ocean. In fact, I knew your mother personally."

Relief or *rejection*, those were the emotions Ocean was prepared to feel, but *confusion* had not been on the agenda for that evening, yet—here it was. Max was proving to be a complete anomaly as far as Ocean was concerned. She was usually able to spot *old money, new money* type people from at least twenty paces away, she could discern self-made moguls from trust fund babies in a five-minute conversation, but Max, he was in a class all his own. This man who loved American Soul, greasy Chinese food, walking rather than being chauffeured, this man who was sitting across from her in a pair of twenty-dollar gray sweat pants and a plain white tee—he completely confounded her. "You already knew? Wait—you said, you knew my mother, *personally?*"

Max quickly threw up his hand in protest and laughed. "Not personally like *intimately* personally, just casually. She was an acquaintance, I guess you could say."

Max got up from the sofa and headed over to the kitchen laughing and shaking his head at the foolish idea he'd thrown out by mistake. "I think we should have some wine."

After returning to the sofa he took a seat even closer to Ocean, closing the space that had been between them. As he slowly filled Ocean's wine glass, he tilted his head to the side and smiled at her.

"Okay, so your mother—I met your mother a while ago. Maritza had a knack for identifying wealthy men. She was very good at what she did. She did express some interest in me for reasons which are obvious, but she gave up pretty quickly on any ambition she had

139

about me—or my money. But whenever I was in town she'd call and we'd talk or chat at parties whenever we happened to be at the same one. She was very entertaining. She's probably the most deceitful and at the same time the most brutally honest person I've ever met. The stories that woman would tell me."

Ocean was completely mesmerized. Never in her life had she heard anyone speak the truth about her mother but speak so positively about her at the same time. She was completely enamored with Max.

After taking a sip of wine Max looked at Ocean and tilted his head from side to side, going back and forth with himself about what else he had to say. "You know this auction is not the first time *you* and *I* spoke either."

"It wasn't?"

"No, it wasn't. It was a few years back, after your mother had given up on me for herself, she told me about you...a prettier version of herself but a lot less *worldly*." Max shut his eyes and laughed as he recalled Maritza describing Ocean to him. "We were at a party and she called you and passed me the phone, and you— when you answered the phone, you very politely told me to go fuck myself."

Hearing the story from Max's viewpoint sent Ocean into a fit of laughter. "Oh my God! I remember that."

"Yes, so that was the first time you and I spoke. Then the second time was when I called Greg's office and you answered—I recognized your voice right away." Max flinched and shrugged his shoulders as he peered at Ocean through narrowed eyes. "Now don't hold it against me, but I Googled you. I wanted to see *why* or *what* brought you to Seattle, and I know because of your mother, there was always some type of story in some tabloid about you because of her and while I don't believe everything that's in them, I've found that on occasion they can be somewhat useful. This particular search proved to be useful. I read about her passing and her debt and the auction and there was a section about how her daughter was now heir to the black widow throne and how the women on the West Side should *beware*, that portion of the article was completely ridiculous, of course."

Ocean dropped her head and did her best to smile away the hurt the article caused her. "So, you saw that, did you?"

"I did and like I said, it's completely ridiculous. You are nothing like your mother and even your mother herself couldn't deny that. So anyway, I heard your voice, I saw the article and then one day I'm out trying to find a wedding gift for Greg and Amelia so I head to this local art auction and who do I see? It was like serendipity was a stick that was a beating me over the head. So—I decided to lend fate a hand and I outbid you… on purpose. Silly me, I thought me having the portrait would be a good icebreaker, but—"

"I told you to fuck off…again" Sadness had completely subsided and Ocean was in hysterics. "I am so sorry, I can't believe you still wanted to get to know me after all that; my mother, the article… my big mouth."

Max couldn't help but laugh with her at this point. "I don't know—it's just something about you. You make me smile. You make me happy and I don't know why; but what I do know is, it's not a bad thing."

CHAPTER TWENTY-TWO

Two weeks had passed since Ocean had confessed the truth of her past to both Max and Jentri and she couldn't have been happier. Things between her and Greg had changed as well. Where Greg was once condescending and overbearing, he was now dismissive and guarded. Ocean admired how he looked out for Max and how fiercely he protected him but she resented his implication, rather his outright accusation that she was the someone Max needed protection from.

It was a week before Christmas and despite the fact that the office was going to be open for two days the following week, the partners of the law firm decided that, that Friday evening, the week before Christmas would be the best time to have the office Christmas party, All the partners were there that evening as well as all the junior staffers and in addition to them some of the more important clients were there. Of course, Max had been invited by the partners, Greg, and even Ocean herself but he declined all three offers; he didn't want to add any awkward tension to Ocean's and Greg's relationship so in his stead Jentri happily accompanied Ocean.

"Wow Ocean. This place looks amazing. Your bosses really went all out." Jentri stood next to Ocean just off the entryway to the building slowly taking in all the lavish décor. The once partially furnished, somewhat cold looking rotunda area was now dripping with sparkling icicles, soft white lights lined the reception area, there were three silver Christmas trees strategically placed throughout; and at the tree's bases several professionally wrapped gifts which were all just empty boxes. Behind the large reception desk was a tower of champagne glasses filled to the brim and an ice sculpture in the shape of a star. The area that had once held the leather benches for perspective clients had become a mingling area for the evening. The marble floor was covered with bright red carpet and at the edge of it sat the mother of all the Christmas trees; big, vibrantly green and completely decked out with ornaments that probably cost more than Ocean received in pay for a week.

"Oh, I don't know, I mean the place looks okay…it's just not my type of Christmas."

Jentri looked at Ocean and frowned. "Looks *okay*? Seriously? This place is gorgeous. So, tell me, what's *your* type of Christmas look like?

"It's not so much what it *looks* like, it's more so what it *feels* like."

"Which is?"

"Warm. Warm and inviting."

"And your Christmases in New York, they were warm and inviting?"

Ocean smiled and gave Jentri a gentle nudge. "Christmas itself in New York is warm and inviting. I don't know how to explain it. It's just something about the steam and the smell of hot dogs and chestnuts and the music and the people—the people are always less cold and less cruel at Christmas, I don't know. I guess you just have to be there."

Jentri didn't understand so she shrugged it off. After checking their coats and heading towards the champagne the two women decided to post up by the seafood buffet, rather, Ocean decided they'd post up by the seafood buffet.

"Ocean, do we really have to stand here? I'm gonna start to stink like fish." Jentri sighed as she smoothed down the sides of her formfitting burgundy red satin dress.

Ocean tried not to laugh at Jentri's sulking as she covered her hand over her mouth trying to hide the handful of cocktail shrimp she'd just shoved inside. "You wanna go over by the desserts?"

Jentri rolled her eyes and smiled. "How about the bar?"

Ocean didn't care where they stood. She quickly tossed some more shrimp onto her hors d'oeuvre plate, grabbed her champagne and followed behind Jentri, who was already almost at the bar.

No sooner than they arrived at the bar did Leland Collins approach. "Hello Ocean, so glad to see you could make it this evening."

Ocean quickly freed her hand so that she could shake his. "Hello, Mr. Collins. Thank you, yes, I'm happy to be here." Not wanting to be rude Ocean quickly laid her hand on Jentri's shoulder and smiled. "This is my friend Jentri, she came with me this evening. Jentri McDavid, Mr. Leland Collins."

Leland quickly took Jentri's hand and shook it. The old man was practically salivating but who could blame him? Jentri had always taken a lot of time and care where her looks were concerned but this evening she'd gone above and beyond anything Ocean had ever seen her do. While it was Jentri's habit to typically dress sexy—sexy was her thing; but this evening, she put all her previous themed ensembles to shame. Tonight, she combined her sexy with a little bit of fantasy which if you were a heterosexual male you couldn't help but notice. Hell, if you were *breathing* you couldn't help but notice. Her red dress was adorned with a thin silver chain which hung—rather, it dripped like an icicle from her waist. Her earrings were the perfect size and if you got close enough you could see they were actually tiny little springs of mistletoe. Her hair was pulled back into a tight bun with big bouncy curls sitting at the top of her head and the bun was tied with a red velvet ribbon which she contrasted perfectly with her bright red lips and exaggerated smoky eye. Even her shoes fit her sexy fantasy. Her shoes were patent leather Christian Louboutin pumps. And, in case you missed the subtlety of her earrings, clasped gently around her ankle hung a beautiful bracelet sparking with a diamond mistletoe design.

"Ms. McDavid, very nice to meet you. "Leland's eyes sparkled as bright as a five-year-old on Christmas morning.

"Please, call me Jentri."

Leland wet his lips and leaned on the bar. "Okay, Jentri. So, you're a friend of Ocean's? You have very good taste. This young lady here is quickly becoming one of my favorite team members."

At that point Ocean was only half listening, she'd turned her attention to her half empty hors d'oeuvre plate. She liked Leland a lot, he'd always been nice to her. He checked in on her to make sure things were copasetic between her and Greg but she hated watching married men flirt no matter who it was. Rather than write Leland off and move away as quickly as possible, which is what she normally did in these situations, she decided instead to give him the benefit of the doubt and chalk the whole thing up to Jentri just being Jentri and Leland just being a guy in search of a good ego stroke. She listened but she didn't watch. "Thank you, Mr. Collins. I love working here with you guys and you are definitely my favorite person in the entire building. I mean that."

"Aw, you're a sweetheart Ocean. Thank you." Leland winked at Ocean. "Well ladies, if you don't mind, I'm going to excuse myself now and go mingle with the rest of the guests. Jentri, my dear, it was a pleasure to meet you. Ocean, always a pleasure to see you. I'll try and catch up with you two later in the evening if I can. If not, please have a wonderful evening."

Jentri turned to Ocean and smiled deviously. "He's cute."

"He's married. Did you miss the ring?"

Jentri frowned and leaned back against the bar, slowly swiveling her head around searching the room for another prospect. It wasn't too long before a very well dressed, dark haired gentlemen caught her eye and began to make his approach, the only problem was some thin blonde was trailing behind him the entire way.

"Oceana."

"Mr. Edwards, Amelia—I mean, Ms. Walcott, good evening." Ocean had been having an okay time at the party, Leland drooling on Jentri aside, but now she had a sinking feeling her night was about to be soured. "Mr.

Edwards, this is my friend Jentri McDavid. Jentri this is Gregory Edwards and Amelia Walcott."

Neither Greg or Amelia extended their hands towards Jentri, Greg stared and Amelia forced a fake smile and twisted the engagement ring on her boney little finger. "Jentri, is it?"

"Yes, Jentri McDavid." Jentri was no slouch in the condescension department, she gave just as good as she received and her fake smile was plastered firmer and wider than Amelia's. "Amelia Walcott. I believe I've heard of you."

Amelia chuckled. "I don't see how, I don't do much socializing. I'm a corporate attorney—always busy. Maybe you've done work for my firm. Are you a temp like Oceana?"

As she straightened her dress which didn't need straightening, Jentri smiled and chuckled back at Amelia and casually shook her head no. "No, no, I'm not a temp but I'm certain I've heard of you—your father, that's it. Your father and I are old acquaintances. Yes, that's it. And I believe he mentioned you a time or two."

"My father. I don't think so. You must have me confused with someone else." The ring twisting had ceased and now Amelia's hands were clasped defiantly in front of her.

Jentri tilted her head and looked off into space as if trying to recall a memory, a memory Ocean knew was already at the tip of her tongue. "No, I only know one Walcott. You kind of look like him. He's retired now, right? Now, if I remember correctly, you took over his old position at his firm, isn't that right? How is he doing? It's been ages since he and I spoke last."

"He's fine." Amelia had clearly lost this skirmish and was not happy about it. "Gregory, I'm going to go have a chat with Leland. Find me when you're done here."

Now it was down to just the three of them but Greg was clearly disinterested in Jentri, her looks and her personality, so she leaned back against the bar and went back to scanning the room. As disinterested in Jentri as Greg was, Ocean was equally disinterested in him, if not more.

"Oceana, where's Max this evening?"

Surprised he had broached the subject so quickly, Ocean found herself caught a little off guard. "He's at home. I'm meeting him later and we're going to decorate his place for Christmas."

"Decorating his place for Christmas… sounds like things are getting serious. You don't think you two are moving kind of fast?"

Truth was that from the outside looking in, Ocean knew her relationship with Max was moving at an accelerated pace but for the two of them it was like they'd known each other forever. "No, I don't think we're moving fast at all."

Apparently, Greg had picked this evening to have his condescension make a comeback and put his dismissive attitude on a shelf. "Geesh, at this rate, you'll be all moved in and marking your territory by Christmas."

Maybe he was drunk. Intoxication was the only thing Ocean could think of that would make Greg so obviously rude to her in mixed company, usually his rudeness was hidden in subtext. Tonight, however, the pig of propaganda was lipstick free. Ocean was pissed. "Excuse me?"

Before Greg could respond or Ocean could say anything else, Jentri who was already dressed to kill decided to take on this fight for Ocean too and she slowly skirted her way in between the two. "Mr. Edwards, that was quite rude." Jentri paused and turned her head towards Amelia across the room and raised an eyebrow in her direction. "*You* may choose to form relationships with corrupt little social climbers but I assure you, *Ocean* is nothing of the sort. She prefers to work for what she has, she's not looking for anyone to bankroll her life or pad the reference section of her resume. Your friend is a big boy, I'm sure he can take care of himself. I feel pretty confident in saying that he didn't reach the status he's at in life by making dumb decisions. He seems to be very intelligent and your very intelligent friend has made the decision to be with Ocean. From where I stand, *he* should be the one concerned about *your* decision-making process—not the other way around, and instead of watching his finances you may want to take inventory of your own."

In that moment Greg's eyes looked like they might shatter they were so cold. "And what the hell is that supposed to mean, Ms. McDavid?"

"Well, like I said, Mr. Walcott was an acquaintance of mine for quite a while and…we talked. We talked about places we've been, things we've seen, people we knew. He talked about his daughter quite a bit and I'm just saying—*Max* doesn't need to worry about who he's chosen to be with. And, for the record, the two of them spend so much time together it's like they're practically living together now. Him giving her a key would just be a formality."

Ocean cleared her throat and quickly stuck her head over Jentri's shoulder. "Actually—I have a key."

Jentri chuckled. "See there…looks like Christmas came early."

Round two went to Jentri. Greg's fists were balled up so hard that as he was walking away his hands were turning purple.

CHAPTER TWENTY-THREE

The Tuesday following the Christmas party, the last work day before the Christmas vacation, Ocean had moved the last of her things into Max's townhome.

"This is crazy, two months...*two months* of dating and we're already moved in together. This is insane."

Max laughed. "Yeah, like I said, people say I'm a little nuts."

In the living room cuddled up on the sofa together casually sipping eggnog like they'd done this very thing together for years, Ocean couldn't picture a more perfect way to spend Christmas. "We should go skating tomorrow."

"Can't. We've got plans."

Ocean sat up and looked at Max suspiciously. "Do we now?"

"Yes, we do." Max returned Ocean's suspicious stare with a Cheshire smile. "We're going out of town."

"And just where are *we* going?"

Wanting to let anticipation build as much as he could, Max slowly sipped his eggnog and then set the stage by clearing his throat. "I was thinking we'd do Christmas in New York. You know, Rockefeller Center—ice skating, roasted chestnuts…all that jazz."

Ocean was speechless. She threw her arms around Max's neck and hugged him as tightly as she could.

***

Christmas Eve in New York City and the air smelled like Christmas. After checking into their room at the Waldorf-Astoria Hotel, they immediately made their way to Rockefeller Center. It was the perfect late afternoon. The sun was starting to set, the air was filled with steam, spices, and carols, and Ocean was walking down the street holding hands with the man she'd fallen head over heels with; the same streets she once walked feeling isolated and lonely. Even the pavement beneath her feet felt different.

As they entered the skating arena Ocean was suddenly flooded with familiar feelings of isolation and panic. She felt that everyone in the area was staring at her and the sound of *whispering* voices began to flood out the caroling. She should have known better. Christmas was usually the time when everyone who knew of her was too busy to pay her any attention, but showing up after all these months and with a man, no less—she'd just given the Upper West Side a hell of a Christmas gift… gossip for an eternity.

Sensing what it was she was feeling, Max stepped in front of Ocean and gently lifted her head. "You are *not* your mother, and you are certainly *not* inferior to any of these busybodies. Don't you dare look down."

The sound of Mariah Carey singing *O Come All Ye Faithful* quickly drowned out the murmured voices and Max smiling down at her warmed her from the inside out. "Shall we skate?"

"We shall."

Ocean was having the time of her life on the ice with Max. They must have skated around the rink a good five or six times before Max jumped in front of her and slowly started skating backwards.

"So, I was thinking—"

Ocean smiled and kept skating towards him. "What were you thinking?"

Max grabbed Ocean's hands and kept skating. "You know how everyone here is always talking about you because of your mother?"

"Yeah."

"Well, I think if they're gonna talk about you, it's about time you give them something to talk about." Before Ocean could respond Max had her by both hands and was slowly spinning her around the ice as he slowly dropped to one knee. "Marry me, Ocean."

Ocean was frozen, completely paralyzed with disbelief. "A little caught up in the moment I see."

Max smiled as he released her right hand so he could retrieve a small satin box from his pocket. "No, I'm not caught up in the moment, I'm completely taken with you. I love you Ocean. Marry me."

***

"So—what do you normally do for New Year's?" In the middle of the floor of *their* townhome, Ocean fluffed the pillows surrounding her and Max. Ocean had already decided that nothing they did for New Year's Eve would top the perfect proposal moment she had at Rockefeller Center... so why try? Instead the two decided on a quiet New Year's Eve celebration with just the two of them. A small carpet picnic, good champagne and good music. There couldn't have been a couple more perfect for each other than them. Two silver spoon-fed kids so humble you'd think they'd been raised by saints. They had a shared belief that a good life couldn't be bought with money but could be attained and enjoyed through good food, beautiful art, and soulful music. Neither could think of a better way to bring in the New Year than at home alone with each other surrounded by what and who they loved, truly enjoying *the good life*.

"I usually spend New Year's Eve with Greg. I invited him over but he decided to pass."

"I *wonder* why?" Ocean furrowed her brows at Max and squinted her eyes.

Max sighed as he leaned in to give Ocean a small kiss on the neck. "He'll come around. He doesn't have a choice. We're getting married. He'll come around. He's just really protective of me is all. We're really protective of each other."

"What's that supposed to mean?"

Max took a bite out of one of the chocolate dipped strawberries and shut his eyes as he searched for an explanation. "Let's just say, I'm not overly fond of *his* fiancée. He could do better. He *deserves* better. I know how he must seem to you right now with the things he's saying and the way he's been acting, but Greg truly is a great guy. He's just fiercely protective, but—you couldn't have a better champion in your corner."

Ocean let out a nervous cough and took a deep breath. "Speaking of protection—you and I haven't had the best track record in that area and well..." As she cleared her throat, Ocean looked down at her fidgeting fingers too terrified to look up. "I'm pregnant."

"You're pregnant?"

"I'm pregnant." Unable to discern the tone of his voice right away Ocean kept her eyes cast downward. "I know we didn't talk about this. I can just imagine what

Greg will say. If you don't want me to...I mean, I can...I—"

Max gently took Ocean by the chin and brought her eyes back up to his smiling face. "*Never* look down, remember? You have nothing to be ashamed about and who cares what Greg thinks. Like I said, *he'll come around*. Ocean, me loving you is *not* a bad thing; and *this*—you being pregnant, a new life, one created by me and you...it's a good thing. All is well, Ocean. Life is good."

CHAPTER TWENTY-FOUR

For the first time in his adult life Greg was spending New Year's Eve alone. It was by his own choice, but in truth he really didn't feel like he had much of a choice. It was either subject himself to a night of endless scrutiny and mockery with Amelia and her father or share his best friend with the floozy encroaching on their friendship. He decided neither option was appealing, so he declined both invitations. Instead of being out ringing in the New Year happily, he was sitting at a bar downtown alone trying to drink away the past few months.

He should have been happy, his friend was happy, he and Amelia were getting married soon, and he'd brought in more clients this year than any other attorney at his firm. He should have been happy but when he looked at his reflection in the mirror behind the bar, he couldn't even remember what his face looked like when he felt that way...happy.

As he sat there sulking and staring into the drunken pair of eyes glaring back at him, he became so preoccupied with himself that he hardly noticed when Jentri walked up and took a seat beside him.

"Funny seeing you here alone on New Year's. Where's your *fiancée*?" Jentri hadn't come to fight, so she quickly dismissed Greg's grunt of a response. "No party tonight? What about a New Year's resolution?"

Annoyed by the invasion to his solitude Greg turned giving Jentri a look of pure disgust as he sipped his whiskey and shook off her question. "Why are you here?"

"I'm meeting someone."

Greg laughed and took another sip of his whiskey. "And this *someone*, he wouldn't happen to be from my firm, would he? Isn't that why you came to the Christmas party dressed like that? You were hoping to meet *someone*?"

Jentri smiled as she signaled the bartender. "A lady never tells, Mr. Edwards."

"Is that so? Well then, *you* should have no problem laying all your cards out then." This particular bar was one often frequented by lawyers and stockbrokers. Half the people on Greg's staff stopped in there several times a week for a drink. The odds that Jentri was meeting with someone he worked with were more than likely; he surely wouldn't wager against it. It was more likely that evening that he'd see Jentri with one of his married colleagues than he be awake to see the ball drop. "So, who is it?"

Smiling as she gently twirled the tiny skewer holding the olives in her Martini, Jentri coyly gazed at Greg and pretended not to hear him. "Where's Amelia this evening? Don't tell me there's trouble in paradise already?"

Greg shoved his empty glass towards the bartended as he turned to face Jentri. "What is that, huh? What is it you think you know? Henry Walcott thinks the sun rises and shines out of his daughter's ass; he'd never say one thing bad against Amelia. You're nothing but a con artist. Some wanna be *madam* looking for a foot in the door to a large payday."

While she hadn't come over to be mean, she also hadn't come to be insulted. "You and Amelia, you've known each other since you were teenagers, right? And despite your efforts back then she would never give you the time of day." Jentri slowly sipped her martini, letting Greg twist in the wind a little. "Then out of the blue one day she calls to *talk*, you'd been *on her mind* and she wanted to *catch up*, is that right? Around this same time, you were just joining your firm and bringing with you the one account everyone wanted and no one could get... Maxwell Prentiss. Now let's see if memory serves me correctly. According to Henry, Maxwell wasn't the first Prentiss his daughter had taken an interest in, and while you're not an actual Prentiss yourself, you're the closest thing to a real Prentiss, Amelia could manage to snag. Maxwell's wealth and business sense are as legendary as his reputation for integrity and loyalty and there isn't a person on this earth that Maxwell is more loyal to than you...not even my dear sweet Ocean can compete with you. So, it appears even though she wasn't able to take home the *cash cow* she still found a way to milk it."

It could have been the whiskey or it could have been his mood, or it could have been both, but in truth it was the accuracy of Jentri's assertions that kept Greg quiet.

Jentri knew at that moment that she'd won that fight with Greg but unlike Ocean she wasn't opposed to kicking a man while he was down, especially if that man had pissed her off. "Tell me Mr. Edwards, is it true Max's father left you some money in his will? Rumor has it, that money put you though law school, paid all your expenses so that you didn't have to take out any loans or work and there was still some to spare. Must have been quite the little nest egg. Which reminds me, I've been so rude, I forgot to ask how all the wedding planning is going. I hear you and Amelia's wedding will be quite the extravagant event." Jentri smiled and winked at Greg's reflection in the mirror behind the bar as she spoke. "Do yourself a favor Mr. Edwards, when you and your soon-to-be wifey are out picking out candelabras, try pricing some nice milking pans too. From what I hear, you're gonna need one."

Shock and appall would have been proper feelings to have in that moment, instead Greg was numb. He was numb that is until he looked in the mirror and turned his attention away from Jentri and in the mirror's reflection, waving Jentri over in his direction he saw, Leland Collins.

Leland seemed to be trying to hurry Jentri along before Greg turned around and saw him. The old man had no idea he'd been spotted already and neither did Jentri…not that she really cared.

With the last of her martini gone, Jentri slid her glass towards the bartender and slid down off her seat and smiled one last time at Greg. "Well Mr. Edwards, it's been wonderful running into you again. Enjoy the rest of your evening."

CHAPTER TWENTY-FIVE

"Gregory, get up. What are you still doing in the bed? We're going to be late. Gregory!" Annoyed, Amelia stomped into the walk-in closet and flipped on the lights. "Gregory!"

"Would you *please* stop screaming. I can hear you just fine." Laying on his back with his eyes still closed Greg reached up and ran his hands through his hair and moaned. "Late for what?"

Stomping out the closet with one Milano in her hand, Amelia scowled at Greg in disbelief. "*Late for what*? For brunch, Gregory. Did you forget we're meeting my father and stepmother for brunch today? I think we should seriously discuss your drinking before we get married. I'm not signing on to spend the rest of my life with a drunk."

"*Signing on*?" Greg chuckled as he rolled over and commanded his body into an upright position.

"Are you laughing? This isn't funny, Gregory. How much did you have to drink last night, anyway? Clearly it was enough to make you forget your obligations for today."

Trying to climb out of the whiskey hangover that Amelia's sharp, annoying voice was exacerbating, Greg slowly fumbled his way towards the bathroom. "No

Amelia, it's definitely not funny...nothing's funny."
After emptying his bladder for what seemed like an
eternity, tired of listening to Amelia chastise him
through the wall Greg turned on the shower and stepped
directly under the forceful spray which pounding sound
proved to be just enough to grant him just a little bit of
peace.

Despite the lack of recognition and admiration, Greg
was just as loyal as Max, Greg wanted to spend more
time in the shower but his prior commitment brought
him out. After he was dressed he headed into the
kitchen where he could hear Amelia clicking away on
her laptop. "What time is this brunch, anyway?"

Still annoyed, Amelia sighed but didn't bother to turn
around. "One o'clock."

Confused, Greg glanced at the clock then at the back of
Amelia's head, then back and forth again. "Amelia, are
you serious? It's not even eleven o' clock yet. What the
hell did you wake me up for?"

"What? Were you just planning to lay in bed all
morning? Don't be ridiculous Gregory. You'll never
make partner at your firm if you start developing those
types of habits."

He didn't want to fight, especially not before having at
least one sip of coffee, which he'd hoped would have
been waiting for him when he got out the shower, but it

wasn't, so he made it himself. Coffee in hand and his mind finally deciding to take itself off snooze, Greg sat down across the table from Amelia. "I've been thinking about the wedding."

Listening but not giving Greg her full attention, Amelia kept clicking away. "Yes?

"I've been thinking it's coming soon, so we should probably start working on our vows."

Amelia stopped typing and looked up at Greg as if she were waiting on the punch line. "*Vows*? Why would we write our own vows, Gregory? That's the minister's job."

"Lots of couples write their own vows, Amelia. It's a lot more common than using standard text."

Amelia scoffed. "It's probably common among common people having their sad little common ceremonies. Our wedding will be anything but *common*. Besides, we're both busy people, we don't have time for such silly things. I mean really, what would we say?"

Greg sipped his coffee and gazed across the table at his soon to be wife. "Amelia, I've been obsessed with you since I was a teenager. If the wedding took place tomorrow, I know exactly what I would say."

CHAPTER TWENTY-SIX

The first working day after New Year's was going a lot better than Ocean thought it would. That Tuesday morning, she braced herself for every and any dig coming her way from Greg, but by two o'clock there hadn't been any. Thankfully, Greg had spent all morning in his office behind closed doors. Ocean was no fool she knew it wasn't because he was still licking his wounds from the run in he had with Jentri at the Christmas party. Greg's seclusion was due to a visit he had with Leland Collins. Ocean was thankful to Leland that morning, she knew his unannounced presence would annoy Greg so much that he'd be too distracted to bother her and she was in desperate need of a slow quiet day. Morning sickness was hard enough on its own but Greg berating her would have just added to the misery.

The afternoon couldn't pass quick enough for Ocean, three more hours and she was out the door. Per their previous talk, Ocean had automatically gone back to her old hours—no more staying late or coming early, not only because she didn't want to and they'd already agreed to an end date on the extended hours, but because physically she didn't think she'd be able to. Her morning sickness had her in and out the bathroom all day.

Unfortunately for Ocean as she was walking back to her desk coming from her fifth bathroom break that day, she could hear Greg's voice coming from the intercom, and he was requesting her presence in his office.

Inside Greg's office she didn't stand like she usually did, she immediately walked over to the empty chair opposite him and took a seat. "You needed to see me, Mr. Edwards?"

Clearly still in a foul mood from whatever unpleasant conversation he had with Leland that morning, Greg barely glanced at Ocean as he thumbed through the stack of papers he had in front of him. "Yes, Oceana. I know we agreed your extended hours would last until the New Year, but I need you to commit to staying until six every evening just a while longer."

"I can't."

"You can't?" Greg stopped thumbing and looked at Ocean then bolted to his feet. "What's that? What the hell is that?"

Confused Ocean looked around the room then searched the floor in front of her before finally realizing he was staring at her engagement ring. "Oh."

"*Oh*? Oh, is all you have to say? What the hell do you think you're doing?" Greg was pissed. As he paced the area behind his desk rubbing and shaking his head, his glare never left Ocean's hand.

Ocean was completely shocked at Greg's response. She half expected him to come around the desk and pull the ring off her finger. "I…I thought Max told you."

Greg stopped and looked at Ocean in the eye and scowled at her. "No. No, Max definitely did *not* tell me."

While she was hesitant to proceed at that point Ocean knew Greg wanted more. "He proposed on Christmas Eve in New York and I said, yes. We're getting married in—"

Greg threw his hand up cutting Ocean's statement off. "No. No you're definitely not getting married, whatever plans you had, whatever game you're playing—it will not end up with you as the new Mrs. Maxwell Prentiss."

"That's not your call!" Now Ocean was pissed and nausea be damned, she got up and moved closer to Greg, she was not going to just sit there and take his shit. "You do not get to tell me how to live my life. Max asked and I accepted. Your approval isn't needed and I don't remember it being requested."

"You scheming, conniving whore. I won't let you do this, even if it means showing up at your wedding just to I can object. No minister is going to marry some Mata Hari reincarnate who's only out to get rich." Pacing back and forth and pulling his hair proved not to be enough of a release for Greg and in a fit of anger he knocked everything off his desk...computer and all.

Ocean had enough as well, she knew exactly who her mother was and what she did, but Greg's constant insults were becoming more than she could bear. At least the yentas on the Upper West Side had enough decency to whisper behind her back. Unfortunately, before she could let him *have it*, she very literally let him have it and threw up all over his newly cleared off desk.

Greg looked down at his vomit filled desk with disgust then back at Ocean, then her ring, then finally up at the ceiling and shook his head with dismay. "Let me guess...you're pregnant—aren't you?"-

CHAPTER TWENTY-SEVEN

"You're home early." Max peeked over the sofa in the living room then quickly got to his feet to greet Ocean.

"Yeah, I got fired...or maybe I quit. I'm not really sure which." Feeling very empty and very much defeated at that moment, Ocean let her head fall on Max's chest.

"Sounds like you and Greg had an exciting day." Max wrapped his arms around Ocean and slowly rocked her from side to side.

"You could say that. He yelled at me and then I threw up on his desk."

Max couldn't contain his laughter. "You threw up on his desk?"

Ocean couldn't help but giggle herself at the ridiculousness of it all. "Yeah, I showed him, huh?" Still giggling Ocean lifted her head and looked at Max with her big sad brown eyes and pouty face. "He already hated me—he probably wants to kill me now."

"He doesn't hate you, he just doesn't know you. I'm telling you, he'll come around. He'll get to know you and when he does, he will love you." Max walked slowly with Ocean tucked closely to his side and his arm around her back. "How about you take a quick shower and try and relax and I'll make you some soup and then you can tell me what the fight was all about."

Ocean couldn't deny that the shower Max suggested helped her relax. Once out of the shower the aroma of chicken noodle soup was so alluring she decided not to waste time getting changed, she tied up her bathrobe and shoved her feet into her pink fuzzy slippers and headed to the kitchen.

At the sound of shuffling feet, Max glanced over his shoulder and smiled at Ocean, whose nose was leading the way into the kitchen. "I take it you're hungry?"

Ocean raised her eyebrows and smiled as she sat on the barstool she'd pulled out from under the island in the middle of the kitchen where her soup was waiting. "Starving."

"Well now, let's see, you mentioned something about Greg yelling... you must have really gotten under his skin today. Greg is not a yeller." Max placed a box of saltines on the countertop next to Ocean's soup as he sat down beside her.

"Oh, he yelled today." Ocean quickly blew at the soup on her spoon then just as quickly she shoved it into her mouth. "And, he was pissed off alright, but I didn't actually *do* anything, I was just sitting there, me and my engagement ring and then *boom*! He lost it."

Max flinched and rested his chin on Ocean's shoulder. "I'm sorry. I was going to tell him on New Year's Eve but he didn't come over and I didn't want to tell him on the phone. We're supposed to meet this Friday after he gets off work, I had planned to tell him then. Honestly, the way you two dance around each other and dismiss one another, I didn't think it would come up. When I'm with you, he's the last thing you wanna talk about and vice versa. I'm sorry, I should have told you he didn't know."

"You're forgiven." After giving Max a quick kiss on the nose she pushed her now empty soup bowl away. "I don't get you two. You're so easy going and approachable and fun...I don't think he knows what fun is. He's so—so...I don't know, he just acts like he's so superior to everyone else. He's so stuck up."

As he clasped his hand around hers, Max got up from his seat and began leading Ocean down the hall. "He only seems that way because you don't know him. Greg's definitely a hard person to get to know but once you do get to know him, he's someone you definitely want to keep in your life. I'm gonna give you a glimpse of the real Greg."

Down in the basement, in a room that looked a lot like a blues lounge, was the area that had been designated to Greg. Ocean studied the black and cobalt blue walls for some kind of indication that she was wrong about Greg. Maybe an old family photo with him smiling and laughing, or some kind of humanitarian certificate, she'd have settled for seeing a baptismal record at that point. "And I don't get why he has a room here. He has his own place, doesn't he?"

As he flipped open a shelf on a large mahogany entertainment center, Max shrugged and took a breath. "There's always a spare room for him wherever I am…I've got a room at his place too. Home for me and Greg isn't a place, it's each other."

Ocean moved in closer to the entertainment cabinet to get a better look at the dozens of jackets sitting on the shelf Max had opened.

Side by side in front of the shelf Max looked down at Ocean and smiled. "Vinyl. He loves vinyl—all American Soul. I never really had a genre preference as far as music was concerned until I met Greg. And no offense to Mr. Sheeran, I loved his concert, I especially loved that little number of his you've been humming around the house since we went to see him."

Ocean gave Max a quick bump with her hip as she started looking through the numerous vinyl jackets on the shelf. "It's hard to believe *Mr. Fancy Pants* likes soul, I pegged him more as the opera, symphony type."

"Well, most people who've experience pain can appreciate soul more than those who haven't, and Greg is very appreciative. It's why he leaves his vinyl's here;

he knows I'll take care of them. There's something in soul music that's soothing to someone who's hurting...I guess it makes them feel less alone."

Ocean stopped looking through Greg's collection and gave Max her undivided attention. In a small love seat pressed up against the wall between Greg's bed and the entertainment center, Ocean curled up against Max and wrapped her arms around his waist and listened.

Max shut his eyes and rubbed Ocean's side as he took a deep breath. He hadn't planned on telling Ocean about how he and Greg met, he didn't feel it was his story to tell, but he knew Greg would never tell her and it was a story she needed to hear. "When Greg and I met, I was fifteen and he was thirteen and he was well on his way to becoming a teenaged gigolo. He was an attractive kid and he knew it. Girls liked him, so he used his looks to his advantage and he took things from them; money, clothes, food, all sorts of things. He didn't attend my school when we met but he was always there hanging around and whenever he showed up a group of girls would always surround him, which made me curious." Max paused and chuckled as he rubbed the side of his face. "It's true what they say about private school girls, they all want to experience a bad boy. Greg happened to be the only available option in the area at the time. He was a good looking kid from the *bad* part of town, who was attractive enough to bring home and meet the parents and pass for a neighborhood kid...once you cleaned him up of course. He took the girls on train rides through the city, managed to get them wine coolers and cigarettes—they all wanted to be *Greg's girl*. So, one day I see him taking money from this girl in my class, a cheerleader, real stuck up bitch. I passed them on the sidewalk on my way home and I pulled him to the side and I tell him, *taking her money only proves that you're worthless*. I honestly didn't mean it the way it came out but before I could explain, he had a fit and kicked my ass."

Ocean sat up and looked at Max in disbelief. "No way. Greg beat you up and you still became friends with him?"

Max laughed and turned sideways to lay his head in Ocean's lap. "Yes, he certainly did. Yeah, so then he ran off. Eventually, maybe a week or so later he comes back to the school and he's waiting for me outside. He came to apologize. I was kind of a sick kid and I guess somebody told him about it, so he came back. I told him I didn't need his pity and he said that was great because he was fresh out. After he apologized he walked me home and I finally got to tell him what I meant by the whole *worthless* comment."

Shaking her head as she looked down at Max and ran her fingers though his hair, Ocean pursed her lips and squinted her eyes in confusion. "So, he beats you up and then you become his friend?"

Max winked at Ocean then shut his eyes and relaxed to the feel of her fingers in his hair. "Besides feeling bad that he beat up a sick kid, he was also worried I'd call the cops and have him arrested. I told him I wouldn't, if he told me what he needed the money for. He decided to show me instead. That afternoon, I went to Greg's apartment in one of the more dangerous parts of Chicago. That was my first encounter with a housing project. As soon as we walked into his apartment, I could hear it."

"Hear what?" Ocean was completely captivated by the story of a life she would have never imagined Greg living.

"Elvis. His mother was playing the Elvis record, *In the Ghetto*. She was sick, Greg's mom, she was dying, I don't know from what but she was dying and Greg was taking care of her. All the money he got from the girls at my school went towards paying the rent for his roach infested apartment, keeping the lights on and food whenever he could manage it. Apparently, once upon a time Greg's mom lived on *my side of the tracks* in a beautiful home with Greg's father. For whatever reason the two never got married and one day he just left her, rather—he put Greg and his mother out and then he went on and married some escort he met in Vegas. He completely cut off Greg and his mother."

Ocean gasped. "So that's why he hates me, because his dad left for someone like my mom."

Max twisted the damp ringlet of hair that hung over Ocean's shoulder. "He doesn't hate you, love. Trust me, he doesn't. Anyhow, with no money and nowhere else to go Greg and his mom moved into the projects and his mom never had a job before so she did what she had to do for money… only no one was polite enough to call her an escort. I guess at some point she caught something from one of her clients, and well—then she was dying. Greg took really good care of her though, made sure she was as comfortable as possible. Music seemed to soothe her. After that first day I went over there, I started stopping by regularly. I used to bring food over and we'd sit and talk and they told me about things they use to do for fun together before his mom got sick, which was mostly music festivals and live bank events. And I told them about my mom and how she used to read to me and write these elaborate stories before she died. I told them about how my mother had killed herself. My mother was so smart, so creative and so sad. She really suffered with depression. After she died, everyone in my neighborhood wrote her off as some selfish nut; but one day at Greg's, sitting on the floor listening to the radio I heard her name—*Mercy Prentiss*. Greg and his mom had called the radio station and asked to have a song dedicated to her, *Beautiful World* by Louis Armstrong…no one before except me and my dad had ever mourned my mother, no one else ever thought she was worth it. These two people never had, and never would meet her, they grieved for my mother."

With his eyes closed Max smiled, it was as if he were smiling right at Mercy in that moment. "Mostly, when I went to Greg's we'd just listen to music. He and his mother both loved music. You could fall in love with a song by just watching them and seeing how much they loved it. And they had an amazing collection. Half the stuff on the shelf here now is from Greg's old apartment in the projects. Of all the music we listened to, they both loved Elvis most of all. There wasn't a day that I stopped by where we didn't listen to *In the Ghetto* at least once. After three months of hanging out and listening to music and laughing together—Greg's mom died. The music seemed sadder without her there to sing along to it, so I told Greg he should come stay with me. Finding Greg was like finding my long-lost brother. There was one night, maybe a year or two after he moved in where I'd gotten sick with the flu or something I don't know, but anyway, Greg stayed up all night with me. He sat on the floor in my bedroom right by my bedside all night checking my temperature, putting damp towels on my forehead—all night long. He just sat there waiting for me to get better—playing his favorite soul music to soothe me. The kid had a heart like a lion. He still does. He doesn't hate you Ocean, he's just trying to protect me. There have always been people in my life who have tried to take advantage of me, especially when I was younger and just taking over my father's business. Even before then, honestly. When I first moved out on my own and went to college—whether it was physical defense or mental strategy, Greg has always been there for me, he's never left my side. It's like he's still sitting on my bedroom floor waiting for my fever to break. But—he doesn't hate you; the stubborn ass just doesn't let anyone get close to him, but don't worry my love, I will get you in. I will crack open that steel wall he's built around himself and I will get you in."

CHAPTER TWENTY-EIGHT

Early on Friday evening sitting across from Greg at their favorite steakhouse, both men seemed to be relieved to finally be in one another's presence. Max lifted his glass towards Greg and nodded. "Over two decades we've known each other and this is the first year we weren't together toasting in the New Year."

Greg raised his glass and quickly took a sip. "You make it sound so ominous."

Max smiled and shrugged. "So, what did you do for New Year's Eve anyway? I know you didn't spend it with Amelia."

"You're an ass." Greg couldn't help but chuckle, Max knew him too well. "I went to the bar around the corner from the office and had a few drinks."

"And that was more fun than hanging out with your brother and celebrating the start of something new?" Max leaned back in his seat and let his hands rest on his thighs as he stared at Greg.

Greg knew exactly where Max was headed with the comment but he decided it was too early in the evening for such serious talk. "Actually, you'll never guess who I ran into at the bar that night. Jentri McDavid. She was there to meet Leland."

Max jolted forward resting his arms on the table. "No— Leland, really?"

Grinning from ear to ear as he sipped his whiskey. Greg couldn't contain how humorous he found the situation. "Yeah, Leland. The old bastard was too much of a coward to come all the way inside the bar so he just stood at the door. He doesn't know I saw him." Greg raised his finger to pause for a moment so he could take another sip. "If he did know that I know, he definitely would not have come to my office earlier this week and insult me about my clientele."

Max shook his head in confusion. "Your *clientele*? What's wrong with your clientele? You bring in more clients than anyone else at that firm."

"But they're all women. He thinks I'm setting a poor tone for myself, that I'm giving myself a *bad reputation*." Greg laughed as he kicked back in his seat recalling the hypocritical lecture from his boss.

"And you didn't call him out? What wrong with you? The Greg I know doesn't stand for such hypocrisy."

Greg shrugged as he gently flicked the bottom of his whiskey glass with his finger. "I don't know, it didn't seem worth it. I had other things on my mind." Suddenly remembering what one of those other things was, Greg sat up and rested his elbow on the table. "Speaking of Jentri McDavid, have you met her?"

"Ocean's friend?" Max furrowed his brow in bewilderment, he could only guess where this was heading and it was definitely to a place he did not want to go.

"Yeah, *Ocean's* friend." Greg rolled his eyes and shook his head in dismay at the mention of Ocean's name.

"No, I haven't met her but Ocean told me about her. I think the term *sugar baby* is what Ocean used to describe her. Apparently, she's really smart. She's got an MBA in Business and a B.S. in Social Science. Highly intelligent but chronically lazy, is what Ocean said. Her whole focus in life is to be a *lady of leisure* and while she was in school she learned that there were a lot of guys out there that would pay a lot of money to have a smart, sexy woman at their side for important events. Ocean said, it's the less arduous way for her to put her education to good use and still get everything she wants."

Greg threw up his hands in frustration. "And Oceana is okay with this? She's okay with befriending a woman whose sole aspiration in life is to be like Maritza Wade?"

Clearly at the *meat* and *potatoes* portion of the conversation Max politely signaled their server to bring two more drinks, which he felt would be needed in case one of them choked on any part of their statements. "No, Ocean is *not* okay with it, but she doesn't condemn her for her choices either. Jentri accepts Ocean exactly how she is—you and I both know how rare it is to find someone who accepts you just as you are…flaws and all. Jentri is the one true friend that Ocean has, outside of me of course. Also, for the past year, basically since they met Jentri was engaged to some stockbroker so Ocean figured the sugar baby lifestyle was behind her, but then the guy broke off their engagement and gave her the boot on Thanksgiving so she's been living at Ocean's apartment."

Practical and rational—Greg hated when Max gave him those types of explanations, how could he argue with that? "Well, it appears the sugar baby is looking for a new sugar daddy and your friend Leland might be it."

The sound of air rolling out from Max's lips provoked laughter from both men. It was now Max throwing his hands up at the table. "I thought Leland was one of the good ones. He and my father were friends for years and you know how my father felt about adulterers—he didn't like them and he didn't associate with them. I guess people aren't always who you think they are."

"Okay, here we go." Greg knew it was coming. Aside from just wanting to see each other and hang out, there were issues that needed to be addressed, mainly the woman that had the two of them oceans apart from one another ideologically. Greg rubbed his hands together and raised his eye brows. "Your *fiancée*. Okay, let's have it."

"She's not what you think. She was actually considering ending things with me just because of the way it looked." Max slowly sipped his whiskey as he remembered Ocean's sad brown eyes trying to tell him farewell.

"Sounds like a con to me." Unimpressed with Ocean's sacrificial moment, Greg snorted and began cutting up his sirloin the waiter had just placed in front of him. "I don't believe she would have actually gone through with it; she was just making you believe she would so you would tell her not to. Apparently it worked. She's good. Almost as good as her mother."

He knew before he sat at the table that getting Greg to lower his defense walls wouldn't be easy but the one thing the two men had in common was how unrelenting they both were. Max leaned forward over the table and laced his fingers together as he slowly rubbed his thumb against the length of his index finger. "She's nothing like Maritza...I knew Maritza, believe me the two are polar opposites. Did you know Ocean used to wash dishes at some late-night Italian restaurant down in Hell's Kitchen in New York?"

Greg stopped chewing for a minute and looked up at Max; he was curious yet skeptical. "So, she had a job, so what? I'm sure at some point in her life Maritza had a job too."

Nearly choking on his whiskey Max waived his hand in the air half choking, half cracking up at the ridiculousness of Greg's statement. "Maritza Wade *was* a job, the only thing that women worked was men and their expense accounts." Still smiling as he finally managed to clear his throat and recompose himself, Max sat back in his seat drawing Greg's attention from his plate to Max's face. "Everyone thinks Maritza disowned Ocean, that there was some scandal, some fallout between them over a man they both wanted for themselves so Maritza threw Ocean out rather then compete with her younger sexier self. It's not true though. After Ocean's father died she spent as little time as she possibly could at home. She was always off in galleries or museums or just wandering about the city. Ocean left home the year she turned eighteen and finished high school. She got a job washing dishes and moved into a one-bedroom apartment which she shared with two other girls who hated her and made her pay the bulk of the rent... but she never went back home. Not until her mother was dead."

The lawyer in Greg wanted to cross examine Ocean on the information. "And Ocean told you this information? Sounds like some sob story just to add credibility to whatever con she's trying to run on you."

Max shook his head and smiled. "No, Maritza told me. She was absolutely sickened by the fact that her *gorgeous daughter who could have any man she wanted was living in filth and washing pots and pans like some degenerate street kid.* She begged Ocean to come home. She even went so far as seeking out wealthy philanthropist type men who were definitely not Maritza's taste but she did it for Ocean's benefit. Maritza never wasted her time on men who she thought might *waste* their money on a good cause instead of her. Ocean isn't who you think she is, which is the only thing she has in common with Mata Hari, by the way. Mata Hari was a courtesan who everyone accused and condemned of being a spy; Ocean is a breathtakingly beautiful woman, but she's no seductress, so quit looking for a firing squad. Ocean isn't looking for a handout, she doesn't want to be kept. The girl's got heart. She's a fighter."

Greg twisted his half empty glass on the table as he pondered everything Max had said. "We shall see, won't we?" Greg sighed as he signaled for another round. "For someone so determined not to turn out like her mother it's astonishing how much they seem to have in common. She's pregnant? You're not even married and she's pregnant?"

Max couldn't help but laugh. "Well, that's just as much my fault as it is hers."

"You don't have to rush things you know." Greg downed the last bit of whiskey and shoved the glass near the edge of the table.

"Time waits for no man. Besides when its right, its right, so why wait?" Max stabbed a piece of broccoli and shook it at Max before popping it into his mouth, "Speaking of which, how are thing with you and Amelia? Still going broke paying for this extravagant wedding?"

"Amelia is used to fine things. I'm just happy I'm in a place where I can provide them to her. If you weren't in such a *rush*, I'm sure she wouldn't mind helping you plan your wedding, too."

Max nodded as he chewed his food giving Greg a *no way in hell* look since he couldn't actually say it in that moment. "You keep asking me, *why Ocean*, as if the two of us together is completely ridiculous, when really it's me who should be asking you why. Why Amelia? She's not good for you, you're better than her. And I'm not sure if you've noticed this but she looks a lot like that escort your dad married. Remember when we tracked him down to get him to sign over those guardianship papers? His wife just sat there staring at you, she never said a word. Amelia looks at you the same way sometimes. I always wondered what it was she was thinking."

"Amelia does not look like that woman." Greg had meant that as a firm statement but it came out more like a confirmation of Max's assertion.

Max scoffed. "Sure, she doesn't. Anyway, enough about your wedding that you've been paying for all year and back to me and mine." Max put down his fork and raised his hand to cover his mouth which was half full with steak. "Since Ocean was relieved of her position this week, or quit, she wasn't really sure which but she was confident she was no longer working for you. Anyway, we've decided to get married next Thursday, so make sure you take off that day."

"Next Thursday! Are you kidding me? You've barely been engaged." Greg threw his linen napkin down on his plate and pushed his food aside.

"The whole point of being engaged is to get married, it would have been rude to just invite her to the courthouse and expect her to say *I do* without proposing properly. So, I proposed, she said, yes; and now we can go get married—next Thursday. Make sure you're free." Max could see Greg was annoyed to the point of speechlessness which amused him and worried him at the same time. Greg always had something to say. "Look, if it makes you feel better we had actually planned on getting married in March but with the sudden free time, I convinced her we should just do it now and spend the next three to four months traveling and doing everything we want before the baby gets here and we'll be stuck in the house." Max raised his glass to Greg and nodded. "Life's too short to play it safe. I'm not gonna sit around and wait because other people think it's the appropriate thing to do. I'm gonna live my life."

***

It was a quarter to eleven that evening when Max got home. When he opened the door, he was met with the sound of piano chords, chords he hadn't heard in a while and he quickly took off his jacket and headed towards the library.

As he stood in the doorway of the library leaning against the inside of the door frame, he silently gazed at Ocean and smiled. Filled with a deep sense of admiration and adoration he slowly made his way over to the piano bench and took a seat next to her.

As Max took his seat, Ocean began singing the chorus to Donnie Hathaway's *A Song for You*. As she played the final chords to the song, she looked at Max and bit her lip and frowned. "I haven't learned all the words yet but I think I got the melody right."

"Yes, you definitely do." Max pointed his fingers at the piano and squinted. "Correct me if I'm wrong but that's *American soul* you were just playing, isn't it?"

Oceana gave Max a playful bump and laughed. "It was. I spent the evening listening to some of Greg's music downstairs, and well—it's official, I'm a convert. His music collection is amazing." Ocean turned sideways and rested her legs across Max's lap and wrapped her arms around his torso. "Well, don't leave me in suspense, what did he say? Is he going to come to the wedding? He's not, is he?" Ocean frowned, her eyebrows looked like two angry caterpillars. "He hates me, doesn't he?"

Max smiled as he leaned in and gave her a kiss. "He doesn't hate you and yes, he's coming to the wedding. I cracked the door for you this evening just like I said I would, now you just have to squeeze your way through."

CHAPTER TWENTY-NINE

"He's marrying the temp?" Disgust spilled from between Amelia's thinly pressed lips. "And, today? He's marrying the temp—*today*? For God's sake. Gregory, why didn't you say anything?"

Greg sat at his kitchen table in his Derek Rose silk pajamas and drank his coffee. "Honestly, I didn't think you would want to come."

Amelia stomped around the condo removing her heels along the way and mumbling under her breath the entire time, her head shaking like an electrified rat. "Of course, I'm coming, Gregory. He's your best friend, I have to be there."

Greg raised an eyebrow as he bit into his toast. "You don't *have* to be there. You're making a bigger fuss about it than they are. It's just a small thing, nothing fancy. They're going to say their *I do's* down at the courthouse then we're gonna go out and have brunch together. It didn't seem like your sort of thing so I didn't mention it."

"Honestly, Gregory, how would that look me not showing up to the wedding?" Distraught Amelia picked up her tablet and started scanning through her calendar. "Okay, I'm good, nothing too serious going on at the office today. They *should* be able to manage without me." Amelia laid her tablet on the table across from

Greg. "And no, it's not my kind of thing, but it's for Maxwell, so of course, I'll attend. I can't believe he's actually going to marry the little gold-digger, and so quickly— Is she pregnant? She's pregnant, isn't she? Oh my God, she's pregnant."

Greg took another bite of his toast and shrugged. "Yeah—but they're happy about it. There leaving for four months right after the wedding to travel together. They're happy—*he's* happy. So, I'm *happy* for them."

Amelia growled and shook her head. "That manipulative, money grubbing bitch is going to ruin him. She's going to break his heart."

Greg frowned as Amelia spoke and he tried to discern what that look in her eye and tone in her voice was, and then suddenly it hit him, it was jealousy…jealousy and longing.

***

By one thirty that Thursday afternoon in January, it was official, Ocean was now Mrs. Maxwell Prentiss. Her reception was like none she'd ever attended; trays of various breakfast foods, surrounded the small party of five; biscuits, crepes, waffles, chicken, fresh fruit, mountains of whipped cream—it was no *Breakfast at Tiffany's* but it fit exactly who Ocean and Greg were and how they felt; decadent, rich, versatile, colorful and above all else happy.

"Okay Ocean—I mean, *Mrs. Prentiss*, I have to admit the breakfast thing is starting to grow on me." Jentri laughed as she stuffed fresh fruit into her crepe. "I really am so happy for you guys. You two are so perfect for each other, I honestly can't think of two other social elites who prefer bargain basement over fine dining and luxury. But somehow you both managed to find each other. Cheers to that."

Everyone raised their glasses to toast the newlyweds. Amelia cleared her throat and turned to Ocean. "And your dress, it's absolutely stunning. That must have been your big splurge. Where'd you get it?"

Ocean looked at Jentri and laughed as she smoothed down her dress before turning to Amelia. "Actually, I got it from this little vintage shop I like to go to back in my old neighborhood." The dress was gorgeous, it was lace and form fitting with a slight flare at the bottom; the antique lace was cream colored and came with matching lace gloves. The dress was regal and elegant with a humble vibe—it was everything that Ocean was. "I just fell in love with it as soon as I tried it on," Ocean said with a smile.

Amelia frowned as she studied the dress further. Jentri and Ocean looked at each other and then at Amelia and laughed. The reception was probably the most unconventional any of them had ever been to, but everyone seemed to be in a truly celebratory spirit, everyone except Amelia.

The reception was the first time Jentri and Max had met, as the two chatted Ocean backed away from the table. "Hey Greg, can I talk to you for a sec?"

Greg put down his fork and backed away from the table and stepped to the side to meet Ocean. "Yes—and congratulations by the way."

Ocean offered a small bow of appreciation then reached to the table behind theirs where trays of brunch food sat waiting to be eaten and she pulled a square, neatly wrapped envelope from a bag that was sitting on the table. "I got you this. I know you and I haven't always gotten along and I thought we could start over."

"You got me a gift on your wedding day?" Greg had the envelope partially unwrapped before he froze and then looked up at Ocean in disbelief. He quickly ripped the rest of the wrapping paper off and stared down at the gift in his hands absolutely astonished. "Elvis! You got me a signed Elvis record? Thank you, Ocean."

Ocean smiled and did a slight bounce. "You called me Ocean."

"I don't know what to say, truly—thank you." Greg sat back down in his seat completely mystified.

Max quickly hugged his arm around Ocean's neck after she sat back down then he turned to Greg. "Elvis, huh? Which one did you get?"

Greg looked up confused and then looked at Ocean. "*Can't Help Falling in Love.* So, you didn't help her pick this out?" Greg's eyes darted back and forth in confusion from Ocean to Max then finally landed on Ocean. "You got this for me yourself?"

A signed Elvis vinyl cost a pretty penny, but the check she'd gotten from the lawyer in New York after her father's things were auctioned off paid for it. Ocean had held on to most of the money wanting to use it to buy back her father's art but she didn't have to anymore. She'd splurged on the Ed Sheeran concert, but while the tickets were high, they didn't break the bank. She hadn't wanted to use any of Max's money for anything solely for herself, let alone a gift from her heart to someone else's. "Yeah, I mean, I know you like him…well, Max told me you like him and I figured it was the least I could do after the whole desk incident." Ocean was very pleased with Greg's reaction. He was more gracious to her than she ever thought he could be.

Jentri's laughter quickly broke the mushiness of the moment. "That record probably cost more than your dress."

Ocean picked up a piece of fruit and tossed it at Jentri and laughed. "It was worth every dime *Missy.*"

The sentimental aspect of the gift giving completely eluded Amelia. "Really Gregory, you're an Elvis, fan? Elvis is so—so…*déclassé.*"

The rest of the table went quiet and looked at Greg who was scowling across the table at Amelia, who was too busy picking at her plate of fruit to take note of the fury rising in Greg's eyes.

Ocean laid her head to the side and rested on Max's shoulder and looked up at him. "I don't think I made it completely inside but I did manage to get my foot in the door. Thanks for leaving it cracked for me."

CHAPTER THIRTY

By mid-May, Ocean and Max's world tour was over and they were back at home in Seattle. Nearing the end of her sixth month of pregnancy, Ocean's morning sickness hadn't relented at all, if anything it worsened. Despite numerous bathroom breaks and the perpetual need to take naps throughout the day, their honeymoon had been amazing. They'd managed to stop at nearly every location they had both dreamed of seeing; Rome, Tuscany, Paris, Westminster, and Edinburgh. In each location they'd find the most beautiful spot they could and would take a photo together to commemorate the moment and capture the beauty surrounding them, their happiness, her growing baby bump and just how truly amazing life could be.

When they arrived home Thursday evening, they were both exhausted and went straight to sleep. After they ate breakfast together the next morning Ocean went to take a nap, as per her new routine and jetlag and Max headed out to take care of a few things. It was just about noon that day when Ocean woke up to the sound of the piano playing the same song she was humming in her sleep. When she realized where the music was coming from, she quickly got out of bed, threw on her fuzzy pink robe shoved her swollen feet into her fuzzy pink slippers and headed for the library.

From the piano bench where he sat playing the melody to Ed Sheeran's *Hearts Don't Break Around Here*. Max looked up at Ocean and smiled. After she made her way over to the bench and sat down beside him, he glanced over at her and smiled again. "It just occurred to me, love... I didn't get you a wedding gift."

"So, you're gonna sing to me?" Ocean beamed with excitement, she knew Max had skill on the piano but she didn't think he could sing.

Max shook his head and laughed. "No, darling, I'll leave the singing to you." As he continued to play, he turned his head and gestured toward the handcrafted bookshelf that housed her favorite portrait, her once lost love found again which had proven to be the catalyst of her new love and very happy life.

Ocean looked up and she was stunned, she didn't understand how she didn't see it when she first walked in the room. "Max, it's so beautiful." Above the portrait in a space that looked as if it were made for the framed photo that had been placed there, was a photo of the two of them. They were standing at the top of a hill in Tuscany, his right arm folded across her chest and his left hand resting on her pregnant belly and their heads turned away from the camera looking off into the sunset focusing on the breathtaking view that surrounded them.

Ocean was completely awestruck, she stood there staring at the photo absolutely speechless and started to cry.

As she made her way back to the bench, Max stopped playing and kicked one of his legs around the bench allowing Ocean to back into his arms. "Hey, hey, hey. no crying. If this is what the photo is gonna do to you every time you see it, I'll rip the damn thing down now."

Ocean tried to laugh through but her tears but they kept coming. "No—don't you dare. It's beautiful. It's—it's…"

Max gave Ocean a gently squeeze and kissed the side of her head. "It's *us*…always—and forever. I will *always* have your back. I will always be behind you."

As she wiped the last tear off her cheeks, Ocean sighed as she relaxed to the feel of Max's hand rubbing her stomach and the feel of his breath on her neck. "You promise?"

Max lifted his head from Oceans neck and gently rested his chin on the top of her head. "I promise."

Saturday, in the wee hours of the morning Ocean woke up panic stricken. The entire bed was soak and wet. She quickly reached down with one hand and felt between her legs with her free hand she rubbed her stomach. The feeling of relief that she had that nothing was wrong as far as the baby went was short lived. After verifying the life inside of her was in fact still alive and literally kicking, she looked around for the cause of her soak and wet sheets. It was Max. Max was drenched in sweat and barely breathing.

CHAPTER THIRTY-ONE

At three-thirty a.m. Greg walked into the emergency department of University of Washington Hospital. After speaking with the staff at the nurse's station and obtaining Max's room number he requested an immediate audience with the lead physician assigned to Max and then he headed to the elevator to go and see his friend.

"They won't let me in. I told them—I told them we were married and I'm his wife and they have to let me in…but they won't let me in." Ocean stared at Greg, terrified and confused. She was desperate for his help.

Before he could respond the doctor opened the door to Max's room and peeked his head out and waived Greg in the room. "I'm gonna go check on him and see what's going on and I'll be right out."

Oceans jaw dropped and her eyes glazed over. "You know something, don't you? What is this? What's happening? Why won't they let me in?" Ocean's frustrated pleas proved to be in vain at that moment. Greg cleared his throat and lowered his eyes to the floor, then without a word, he stepped into the room.

It was nine a.m. by the time Max opened his eyes and he smiled knowing he didn't need to look to his left to know that it was Greg who was sitting beside him. "Morning. So, how long was I out?"

"Let's see—Ocean called me screaming on the phone at a quarter to three, so twelve to thirteen hours I'd say." Greg pulled his chair up closer to the bed so Max could see his face without him having to move his head. "She's still out there, you know. And she's pissed, by the way, so thanks for that."

Max laughed and shut his eyes. "I bet she is but it's better this way. You know it is." Max looked at Greg and could see the wheels in his head spinning and him trying to suppress the mounting lump in his throat. "You can't fight this one for me, brother. I know you would if you could but you can't and that's okay."

Greg looked down at Max and nodded as tears streamed down his face. "I'm just not ready yet. I—"

Max took Greg's hand in his and squeezed it best he could. "You've hurt your whole life, you'll get through this just like you got through everything else."

Greg dropped his head and shook it. "No—you pulled me through it. It's different this time, I've got no one now and I don't know how to hurt like this…not on my own."

"You're not alone." Max took a deep breath and looked at the hospital room door. "I was hoping to hang around long enough to meet this child of mine but it seems fate has other plans; ugh, it's probably just as well, something tells me if I'd have lasted long enough to see her, I'd have regrets about letting go. But I know she'll have you, so I'm at peace with not seeing her."

Greg nodded and wiped the tears from his eyes as he stared at the door with Max. "Doc says, at best you've got a couple of weeks left. What do you want me to tell Ocean?"

"The truth…but tell her I love her first, then tell her the truth and let the nurse know it's okay for her to come in."

Ocean jumped to her feet as soon as she heard the door open. She couldn't wait by his bedside but that didn't stop her from waiting by his door. Despite the concerned nurses who tried to convince her to go home and rest, Ocean held her post, pajamas, fuzzy slippers and all. She was physically exhausted but she never moved an inch.

Outside in the hall, face to face with Ocean, whose facial expression said everything her mouth did not, Greg took a breath and looked at the ceiling. "Let's go to the waiting area and talk."

Ocean looked at the door to Max's room then back at Greg. "No! Just say it. Whatever *it* is, just say it."

Greg lowered his head and nodded. "He's dying. He's been dying for a long time now. He was dying the day he met you." Greg quickly reached out to catch Ocean, whose legs betrayed her and he carefully helped her back into her seat. "Cancer. He had it as a kid and fighting it nearly killed him, fighting it also made him miserable. The cancer left him weak and it came back a second time and left him even weaker. He knew if it came around again that he didn't stand a chance and he didn't want to spend whatever time he had left fighting a losing battle. He decided if he was destined to die then he would *really* live first and despite my reservations I've never seen him more alive then when he was with you." Greg looked at Ocean trying to make sure she was okay. She seemed stunned. She was motionless and quiet but he knew she was listening. "No one else knows, except me of course, because he wanted it that way. He thought about telling you but he didn't want to burden you with months of sorrow and agony so he didn't. He wanted to share his life with you, not his death. Personally, as hard as it is for me to say this, I think the fact that you didn't know is probably why he's managed to hold on so long and keep living... he just wasn't ready to let go of the happiness he found with you. Apparently— you make him smile."

The sea of tears that had dammed themselves behind Ocean's red rimmed eyes finally broke free and rushed down her face. She couldn't move, she couldn't speak, she felt as if she couldn't breathe. All she could do was cry.

CHAPTER THIRTY-TWO

Over the next six weeks Ocean managed to convert Max's sterile and cold hospital room into a homey and welcoming place to be. He could have gone home with her but he refused, he wanted the memories that they had in the town house together to be happy ones. So, Ocean brought home to him. She hung some forest green drapes in the windows. She hated the track lighting of the hospital so she brought in two floor lamps with dimming capabilities to give the room just the right glow. She also decided the hospital linens were too thin and scratchy so she brought in a fluffy comforter to keep Max warm and his favorite grey sweat pants, which she probably loved as much as he did. And despite the hospital staff's efforts to stop her she hung pictures all around the room. Pictures of their honeymoon together, pictures of her sonograms which she had blown up and framed, pictures of Greg, and right smack dab in the middle of the wall, the first thing Max saw when he opened his eyes every morning, was the Degas portrait. The hospital staff wasn't at all pleased with the hammering of the nails into the walls but they knew better then to try and piss off a pregnant woman with a hammer who was trying to be brave while her heart was breaking. In the end, the room was so thoughtfully put together, so warm and welcoming all their prior objections fell completely by the wayside.

"How about Maxine?" Laying in the hospital bed next to Max staring at her most recent sonogram, Ocean looked at Max and smiled.

"No, Maxine sounds so old. You can't give her an old lady name, she needs something with more spirit." Max shut his eyes and silently rubbed Ocean's bulging belly as he searched for a name. "How about, Faith?"

Ocean frowned. "No—that makes me think of that George Michaels song."

They both looked at each other and laughed. Max turned his head to Greg who stood quietly in the corner of the room listening to them as he stared out the window. "Hey you, any thoughts?"

Greg leaned against the wall with his arms folded as he watched the sun set. After a few moments of silence, he looked over his shoulder at the two of them and tilted his head to the side. "What about, Mercy—after your mom?"

Max smiled and raised an eyebrow. "What about. Grace—after yours?"

Ocean looked down at her stomach and placed her hand over Max's hand. "What about both? Grace and Mercy...one isn't really complete after all without the other."

Despite the fact that her world was falling apart, Ocean did her best to stay in good spirits. She was at the start of her eighth month of her pregnancy and she wanted so badly for Max to be able to hold their daughter in his arms just one time but she could tell he was getting too tired. Just waking up each day was becoming more and more of a chore and it killed her to know what kind of pain he must have been in each day but he dealt with it and he endured it for her.

Greg and Ocean spent so much time at the hospital that some of the staff thought they were patients. They didn't take shifts, neither left, they both moved their lives into his room to be closer to him. They ate, slept, showered and everything else from that room. Greg hoped that Max would hold on long enough to hold his daughter just once but looking at his friend now, his brother, lying there in his hospital bed that evening in late May, he knew he wouldn't make it. "You okay man? You need more pain meds?"

Max looked at Greg and smiled. "Yeah, but do me a favor first." Max looked down at Ocean and winked. "Put our song on first, will ya?"

Greg walked over to the iPod on the nightstand next to the hospital bed and selected Ed Sheeran's *Hearts Don't Break Around Here*, then he went into the hall to get the nurse to administer some more pain meds.

As the song played Max gently rubbed Ocean's side and softly hummed to the music. Greg returned to the corner of the room and folded his arms and faced the window and cried. Ocean wrapped her arms around Max's waist and held her breath until the humming stopped.

Max fell into a coma that evening and died the next day.

PART FOUR

VIA DOLOROSA

CHAPTER THIRTY-THREE

Three days after Max's passing, Ocean found herself on the footsteps of a small cathedral outside the city. Greg had handled all the funeral arrangements. All Ocean had to do was show up, and she did. Ocean arrived to the church twenty-minutes late in a pair of Max's sweatpants and a v neck tee shirt that clung to her very round stomach.

"There you are Ocean, I was just coming out to call you." Jentri quickly tucked her cell phone back into her purse as she grabbed at the hem on the back of her skirt commanding it not to rise as she took a seat on the steps next to Ocean. "We've been waiting for you, doll. We didn't want to start without you."

Ocean stared at the hearse parked off to the side of the church. Her eyelids were heavy and her normally soft and compelling brown eyes looked like black dots floating in a sea of red. "I'm fine. You can go."

Jentri reached out her arm to caress Ocean but withdrew her hand before she made contact. She knew there wasn't a single conversation or ounce of caress that was going to help her friend through that moment and she refused to insult her by trying.

Jentri got back up, gave the sides of her skirt a tug and silently headed back into the church. No sooner then

Jentri had gently shut the door behind her was it thrown open by Greg.

Greg was pissed, but he'd been pissed off the past two days so not much was alarming about his mood. Only now, now he had a person right in front of him to be pissed off at because it wasn't appropriate for him to be angry with the dead and he fought like hell not to be, but now he didn't have to fight his feelings because he finally had someone tangible to unleash on. Greg looked down at Ocean with disgust and shook his head. "Are you kidding me? You didn't even bother to get dressed? All you had to do was look nice and show up on time and you couldn't even do that!"

With his hands on his hips Greg paced the landing of the church entrance behind Ocean. He knew just by looking at her that Ocean was in no condition to argue with him and he had never before really considered himself to be a bully but in that moment, he was glad she wasn't fighting back; it made him feel good to finally let off a little steam on someone. "I picked the church, I made the phone calls, took care of the limo, flowers, preacher, casket—me, me, *me*! All *you* had to do was get up, get dressed and get here on time. Not only are you late but you look like shit and now you're holding everyone else up because *you* don't want to come in."

Greg's rant was turning into a full-blown tirade. He stopped pacing and stepped down and grabbed Ocean by the arm and pulled her to her feet. With his hand wrapped around her arm and his nose practically touching hers, Greg took a big shaky breath and scowled at Ocean. "You ungrateful little bitch, so help me God, you will get your ass in that church and show my brother the respect he deserves or I will drag your ass in there with me, but you *are* going in."

Ocean was unfazed by the manhandling, in fact she barely noticed it. What distracted her attention away from the hearse and steadied her on her feet was Greg's little monologue. Ocean looked at Greg with her swollen eyes and a lost, spacy look in her gaze and she gathered all the strength she had to take a deep breath. "Respect? Don't you dare lecture me on respect. I sat in that hospital for weeks. I never left his side. I never asked or begged or pleaded him to fight for his life so that I could keep him in mine. I respected him so much that I held my breath while he took the very last of his. Don't you dare lecture *me* on how *I* need to show respect for my *husband*."

Greg released Ocean's arm, but before he could say anything she was walking down the steps and out into the street away from the church. There really wasn't anything he could have said in that moment...she was right. From the second Ocean walked into Max's hospital room she never complained, she never shed a single tear. She wanted to be as brave as she possibly could as she watched him die—as brave as he was as he laid there dying...and she was.

The funeral was brief, just as Max instructed Greg he wanted it to be, no muss no fuss. The funeral invitation list was short, the church was small and the repass was to be quaint and light hearted.

Ocean never entered the church, the next time Greg laid eyes on her was at the cemetery. She was standing underneath a tree about twenty feet away from the burial site hugging herself and swaying from side to side as she watched everyone lay a rose on the casket and say their final goodbyes.

The steakhouse where Max and Greg had so often met up for meals and drinks graciously closed their doors to the public that afternoon and hosted the repass.

"I honestly can't believe it. The least she could have done was pretend that she cared but to just not show up at all—how tactless." Amelia waived her hand around in the air as she sipped her martini and condemned Ocean at the same time.

Greg stood by Amelia's side silently and, much to his surprise, so did Jentri. Greg didn't know much about Jentri but of what he did know of her this was surprising behavior. She didn't say a word as Amelia belittled and admonished her best friend. Realizing Amelia wasn't going to let go of it, Greg cleared his throat and interrupted her soapbox moment. "She was there. Oceana. She was at the church and she was at the cemetery too."

Jentri let out a deep sigh of relief, Greg stared at her confused as to why she hadn't said anything, why she wasn't defending her friend, especially since Jentri had seen her too, Jentri had seen her first.

Amelia clicked her tongue and looked at Leland. "She was probably hoping to go straight to the reading of the will. Speaking of which, Gregory—"

Before Amelia could finish her thought and piss Greg off, he raised his hand in the air balking her as he answered his vibrating phone. "I'll be right there."

"You'll be right where, Gregory?" Obviously annoyed she didn't get to finish her previous statement, Amelia was determined to find out the cause of the intrusion. "You can't just leave. Who was that anyway?"

"The caretaker at the cemetery." Greg shoved his phone back into his pocket and looked at the small group of people surrounding him, after a moment of head swiveling he rested on Jentri. "Did you drive here?"

Jentri looked panic stricken. "Me? Uh—yeah, I got a rental for the day."

Something was off with Jentri but Greg didn't have time to find out what. "I need your keys."

"Is there a problem Gregory? What did the caretaker want?" Amelia set her drink down on the table preparing to leave with him.

Seeing Amelia prepare herself to accompany him surprised Greg, if it hadn't been for her very inappropriate, almost inquiry, he actually might have let her come. "No, you stay here Amelia. I won't be long. Apparently Ocean is still at the cemetery. They can't get her to leave."

Amelia's face twisted in disgust. "And why are they calling you?"

Greg sighed. "Because I'm the one who's been handling everything, Amelia." Greg briefly touched Amelia's arm then took off towards the door.

Back at the cemetery pulled over on the side of the street about ten feet from Max's final resting place, Greg sat in Jentri's rental car trying to figure out what to say to get Ocean to leave. The longer he sat there the more annoyed he got that he was even back there to begin with, and then as if the day couldn't get any more miserable it started to rain. "Just what I fucking needed." Greg slapped the steering wheel then looked over at the spot where Max had been recently lowered into the ground. And there, leaning on the pile of dirt that covered Max's casket sat Ocean.

After two or three more minutes of sitting in frustration he made his way out the car and over to the stubborn pregnant woman who sat there in the pouring rain refusing to leave. Greg looked down at her and realized there was nothing he could say to her in that moment to get her to leave, so he bent down and carefully scooped her up in his arms. As he picked her up and her left hand left the rain soaked earth over the burial site, Ocean released seven weeks' worth of tears all over Greg's shoulder. Her heart wrenching cries almost brought him to his knees.

CHAPTER THIRTY-FOUR

"Mr. Edwards, I know you said not to bother you today and to hold all your calls, but this woman is insistent, Sir. She says it's an emergency." Greg rolled his eyes at his new temp as she timidly hid behind his door and spoke to him. Against his better judgement he'd allowed her to stay in the office today despite the fact that he wasn't taking calls or seeing anyone so there was no real reason for her to be there. His cases had piled up some since he'd been out for so long but he wasn't really all that far behind, he had a habit of working ahead, so him being out hadn't really affected him that much on the professional front. He'd only come in that day because he needed a distraction.

"Well—who is it?" Greg could clearly see the timid little woman was terrified of him and he didn't need to snap at her but he did so anyway.

The woman flinched at his response and hid more of her body behind the door. "It's uh—Jen—Jentri McDavid, Sir."

Confused but also intrigued by the fact that Jentri would have the nerve to call him personally, Greg pushed aside the files in front of him. "Okay, send her call through."

"Good morning, Mr. Edwards, its Jentri. I am so sorry to be bothering you at work but I really don't know who else to call."

Not only had Jentri been acting different but now listening to her on the phone she sounded different too. "Well, what is it you want? What's this *emergency*?"

Jentri nervously cleared her throat. "It's Ocean."

Greg rolled his eyes and sighed. "What now? I dropped her off at home yesterday, I put her in the bed and I even tucked in her God damned covers. Don't tell me she's back at the cemetery again."

"No. Well, I don't know."

Jentri was nervous and even though Greg couldn't see it, he could feel it.

"It's just, I've been trying to check in on her since last night, I've gone by the townhouse three times this morning. I just want to make sure she's okay but I can't get in and she won't answer the door. I'm worried. I was hoping you could come by and just let me in so I can check on her."

"Fine." Greg wasn't exactly sure why he was agreeing but he wasn't sure of all that much anymore. "I'll meet you there in fifteen minutes."

Jentri must have already been at the townhouse when she called Greg at work because it had taken less time than he said; Greg pulled up in front of the townhome in ten minutes and Jentri was already there sitting on the steps waiting for him.

The inside of the townhome was dark and quiet, Jentri followed behind Greg on her tiptoes so that her heels wouldn't disrupt the silence. At the end of the hall inside the master bedroom with the comforter pulled up to her neck, Ocean laid on her side, motionless.

Jentri squatted down next to her and gently brushed the hair away from her face. "Ocean, sweetheart, are you alright?" Jentri searched Ocean's eyes and the empty sad stare that looked back at her concerned her more than Ocean's non-responsiveness. "Ocean, it's Jentri. Ocean, please—say something."

Greg stood by the door silently watching the interaction but unsure of how he felt about it.

Unsuccessful at rousing any kind of response from her friend, Jentri turned and looked at Greg. "Maybe we should call an ambulance?"

Greg pushed himself from the doorframe and walked closer to the bed. "And tell them what, that she's sad? Not really a reason to send out paramedics."

Jentri looked back down at Ocean and shrugged. "Have you ever seen anyone *this* sad before? We can't just leave her here."

"For Christ's sake." Greg put his hands on his hips and quietly studied Ocean for a moment. After brushing Jentri off to the side, he threw the comforter off towards the end of the bed and scooped Ocean up in his arms and headed for the door.

Still in Max's grey sweatpants and v neck tee, Greg wrapped Ocean in a throw blanket he'd grabbed off the sofa on his way out the townhome and wrapped Ocean inside of it and carried her into the emergency room. That afternoon Greg found himself back at the one place he didn't want to be, University of Washington Hospital.

CHAPTER THIRTY-FIVE

"Maxwell's stepmother left you another message today, Gregory, are you ever going to call her back? It's been four days now." Amelia twisted the Cartier bracelet around her wrist as she listened to the message left.

"Eventually. I'm not really in a rush. Seriously the man's been dead less than a week, she needs to calm down."

Joining Greg in the living room but sitting on the accent chair across from him rather then on the sofa next to him, Amelia gave Greg a disappointing look. "She was his mother, Gregory."

"That woman was *not* his mother." Greg got up and went over to the bar cart and poured himself a drink. "What kind of *mother* doesn't know her own kid has cancer?" Greg scoffed as he threw back a shot of whiskey then poured himself a double.

"Really, whiskey? At two in the afternoon?" Amelia's disapproving tone matched her disapproving look perfectly. "You can't blame the women for not knowing Maxwell had cancer. No one knew he had cancer!"

Greg sat back down on the sofa with his drink in hand and stared into the glass. "I knew he had it."

Amelia shook off Greg's response and plastered on the most sincere smile she could. "But really, this isn't standard practice. Maxwell's will should have already been read. What are you waiting for?"

"His wife." Greg took a sip of whiskey then twisted the glass around in his hand.

"Excuse me?" Sincere didn't last long and was an emotion Amelia always had difficult time sustaining anyway. "What are you waiting on her for? She may not have attended the funeral but I'm sure if you told her you were reading the will she'd be front and center."

"Hard to do from a hospital bed, my dear. I dropped her off two days ago. I'm actually headed down there today to see what's going on. The hospital left me a message this morning."

Curious and still very much annoyed, Amelia leaned back in her seat and folded her arms. "You didn't tell me you took her to the hospital, and *why* are they calling *you*?"

Greg was in no mood to argue, he placed his glass on the end table next to him and got up and headed to the kitchen to retrieve his keys. "I don't know Amelia. Anyway, she wasn't doing that great after the funeral and I didn't know what to do with her so I left her at the hospital. She is pregnant, remember? Something could be wrong, I don't know." The more he explained himself the more he eager he was to leave. "Look, I don't know what's going on, I'll go find out and we can talk about it later tonight."

Greg quickly left out the door not giving Amelia a chance to respond. Thirty minutes later he was in the hallway of the hospital outside Ocean's room.

"Mr. Edwards, good to see you, Sir. How are you this afternoon? I'm Mrs. Prentiss's attending physician." The doctor extended his hand to Greg and shook it warmly as he directed him to the nearby waiting area.

"Why did you call *me* doctor?" Still annoyed from his conversation with Amelia, Greg wasn't in the mood for pleasantries.

The doctor quickly rubbed his palms on his thighs then looked at Greg. "Well, Mrs. Prentiss isn't doing well."

Greg shook his head clearly the doctor was misunderstanding him. "No, why *me*? Why did you call *me*?"

Confused the doctor removed his glasses and wiped his forehead. "Well, you're her emergency contact."

Disbelieving the statement he just heard, Greg coughed and stared back at the man. "*I'm* her emergency contact?"

As confused as Greg was now the doctor stared at Greg trying to figure out why he'd be so shocked. "Well— yes. You and Mr. Prentiss, but we knew of Mr. Prentiss' unfortunate passing recently so clearly, we couldn't call him. So, that just leaves you."

Time was not going to minimize the feeling of shock Greg was feeling so he brushed his bewilderment aside for the moment. "Okay, so what's wrong with her? Is the baby okay?"

The doctor nodded. "Yes, the baby is fine."

Greg nodded and threw his hands up in the air. "Okay. So, what is it? What's wrong with her?"

"Takotsubo Cardiomyopathy."

Still not understanding what exactly was wrong Greg stared blankly at the now solemn looking doctor. "And what the hell does that mean?"

Rubbing his chin and briefly staring off into the hallway that led to Ocean's room the doctor then turned to Greg with furrowed brows. "*Broken Heart Syndrome*. It's rare, very rare and can often correct itself but I've never seen such a serious case before. I just don't know if we can do anything for her." The doctor sighed as he clasped his hands together in his lap. "Medicine can fix a lot of things, Mr. Edwards, but we cannot mend a broken heart."

CHAPTER THIRTY-SIX

Taking into consideration Ocean's current circumstances as well as the fact that he already knew what Max's will said, Greg decided on Monday morning, a week after Max's death to just get on with it and read the damn thing.

In the conference room at his firm, Greg sat at the head of the table. With him were Amelia and Leland, and on the phone, was the woman who insisted on trying to pass herself off as Max's mother. Greg wasn't sure why Max's former stepmother insisted on being present for the reading, Max had made it a point not to have anything to do with her after his father died. Despite the fact that she remarried five years ago, the crazy woman kept trying to interfere with Max's affairs and stake claim to the fortune that Max's father had completely left her out of in his own will.

Greg cleared his throat and straightened the papers in his hands. *"I, Maxwell Gabriel Prentiss, being of sound mind and body, do herby declare that this document is my last will and testament. In executing such document, I hereby declare that, 1) I revoke all wills and codicils that have previously been made. 2) I am currently married and after my death will have one living child. 3) I instruct my executor to distribute my estate in the following way: Mrs. Oceana Veritas Prentiss will receive all my liquid assets to include all bank accounts, saving accounts, stocks and bonds—complete collection of art which includes an original Edgar Degas, Rembrandt and Dali. Additionally, she will inherit my classic cars which include a 1966 Ford Mustang Convertible and a 1966 Austin Healey. Gregory Ian Edwards-Prentiss will receive sole and total control of all my existing business and all profits that disseminate from them which include a winery in Napa Valley California, a seafood import/export corporation and a whiskey distillery in Tacoma. Additionally, he will assume ownership of any and all patent and trademarks associated with any and all of the aforementioned business. Oceana Veritas Prentiss and Gregory Ian Edwards-Prentiss shall equally share all rights to my Seattle town home. Should any of the inheritance be unable to inherit for any reason then I give their share of my estate to my one and only child.*

The conference room was uncomfortably quiet until the sound of a slamming phone pierced the air. Apparently, Max's former stepmother had heard enough.

Leland wet his lips and straightened his tie. The man looked as if he'd been submerged in ice water, his face had gone ghostly white; clearly, he was shocked. "Well Gregory, that's quite the gift Maxwell left you, quite the gift. It is also a huge responsibility but don't you worry yourself; I, as well as all the other partners here, will be here to assist you with whatever you might need."

Amelia twisted in her chair smugly smiling at Leland as she did so. "He'll be fine Leland, he has me. Maxwell was no fool, he left the right man in charge. Although, I'm surprised he left all his money to the temp, now *that*, I must say, I do find a little foolish; and to leave nothing to his poor stepmother, nothing. That poor woman."

Greg looked at Amelia as if a second head had just sprouted from her neck. "*Poor woman*? That poor woman tried to have Max declared mentally unstable less than a year ago so she could get her greedy hands on his money. Poor woman, my ass."

Amelia shifted uncomfortably in her seat. "Well, Gregory, she was more of a mother to him than that selfish nut job that killed herself. At least the woman was there for him and his father. Regardless of the fact that she's remarried, she was still a Prentiss—speaking of which, why are you addressed as a Prentiss in the will?"

Greg stood up and snatched the papers off the table and met each inquisitive intrusive glare offered to him by both Amelia and Leland. "Not only are you out of line Amelia, but you are way off base; and don't you *ever* speak of Max's mother *ever again*. As delusional and irrational as some may have *thought* she was, *selfish* was the one thing she was *not*. That woman blamed herself the first time Max got sick with cancer and she made a trade with God to take her instead of her son.

And as deluded as that might be, it is the most selfless thing any one person can do for another. She killed herself to save her son, can you honestly tell me right now in this moment that *your father* would do that for you? And as far as Max addressing me as a Prentiss...he did that because *I am* a Prentiss and have been since the year we met." Disgusted by the responses of all three parties who had attended the reading, Greg shook his head and exited the room.

CHAPTER THIRTY-SEVEN

A week after the will had been read, Greg made another visit to see Ocean at the hospital's insistence. Ocean's state hadn't changed, she wasn't communicating, she wasn't eating and they were preparing to admit her to the psych department if they didn't see a change in the next few days.

Approaching her room Greg could hear a female voice pleading with Ocean, it took him a minute to realize it was Jentri. The tone in her voice gave him pause. Rather than confront her about her change in behavior and try and pull out the information he quietly stood by the door listening to what she had to say.

"Ocean? Ocean it's Jentri. Ocean please answer me. I know this isn't the best time and you're not in the best of places but I need you. I screwed up and I really need you so, please answer me...please. Okay, I know you can hear me, you're not deaf or anything. You're just sad." Jentri took a deep breath and grabbed Ocean's hand and scooted her chair as close as she could to the bed. "Ocean, your inheritance, Max left you all the money he had, Ocean—I need you to agree to not take it all, I need you to..."

"You need her to what?" Infuriated by what he was hearing Greg couldn't stand by his post silently anymore. "What the fuck do you think you're doing? You need her to *what* exactly?"

Embarrassed, shocked and scared Jentri jumped out of her seat and faced Greg. "I—I was uh—"

"You were *uh*, what?"

Try as she might Jentri couldn't shake off the nerves. "I was just checking on her, making sure she was okay."

Greg walked over to the foot of the bed and shoved his hands in his pockets as he studied Jentri. "To check on her? Didn't really sound like that to me. And please explain why it is that she shouldn't take the money Max left for her?"

Jentri stared back at Greg terrified, her mind racing trying to find an answer that would satisfy him, but she couldn't think of anything.

Greg took two slow steps closer to Jentri, his gaze unchanged and his jaw tightening with each step. "Why shouldn't she take it?" When Jentri didn't respond Greg took another step. "Do I need to call the police and tell them how I found you in here trying to extort a grieving widow?"

Jentri threw her hands up in surrender. "No, no. no please, don't."

Greg shrugged and raised an eyebrow as he waited for her to explain. "*Why?*"

"I swear, this isn't my idea. I don't wanna do this. I hate myself for doing this, but—" Jentri paused to catch her breath. Between the nerves and trying to hold back tears she was on the verge of hyperventilating. "Amelia talked to her father about me and somehow she found out about me and Leland and the two of them got together and set me up. They're threatening to file charges against me for prostitution and bribery unless I help them, and I swear I would never intentionally do anything to hurt Ocean, but—"

"*But*, that's exactly what you're doing." Greg stepped back and paced the length of the room rubbing his chin as he tried to process everything Jentri had said. "What kind of charges are they threatening you with, did you say?"

With Greg not taking out his cell phone and dialing the police, Jentri had managed to calm herself down slightly, but not much. "Prostitution and felony extortion, but I swear I wasn't intentionally trying to extort anyone. They twisted my words and made it seem like I was purposely trying to take advantage of people, which is not the case."

Dumbstruck, Greg stopped pacing and turned back to Jentri with a quizzical stare. "Seems like you're not intending to do a lot of things that you are actually doing. This thing with you and Amelia, I know how that started but how does Leland fit in and why would either of them give a rat's ass about trying to set you up?"

Jentri plopped back down in her seat and turned to face Greg. "Well, like I said at the Christmas party, I used to spend time with Amelia's father. And yes, he used to buy me things, but that was all a part of the job, a completely legal job. I joined an escort site to pay off my student loans. I was a sugar baby, that's how I paid my rent and bought nice clothes and everything else I wanted. And *no*, it wasn't a front for prostitution, it really was just dating...at first. There's a lot of rich guys who need dates that are pretty, intelligent, and not looking for a relationship. I did however have two or three clients that wanted more than just a date, and they paid me more. They weren't so much paying for the sex, not really, it was more like they were paying me to be their girlfriend. They treated me like their girlfriend instead of like a hired escort and honestly, I wouldn't have minded being their girlfriend except they were all married. Well—when my fiancé dumped me, I didn't really have anything to fall back on. I had stopped escorting because of him, all my clients had moved on, as they should have, but then around that same time Ocean told me about her mom, Maritza. So, I googled her, I decided instead of joining another escort agency I'd take a beat from Maritza and instead of waiting for men to pick me, I'd go out and pick them. I made a list of potential clients, started working them a little bit, you know flirty phone calls, mid-afternoon lunches, showing up to the same social events...all harmless stuff."

Jentri dropped her head and began fidgeting with her fingers. "And then I met Leland, good old Leland. He wasn't interested in being seduced, he didn't want the long stares across the room or the flirty calls, he *wanted me*; which is what he used to say when he called me. So, I would ask him, what would happen if his wife found out, and he'd make a joke about buying me a flat and shipping me off to Paris and his wife would never know. This went on for days so finally I figured, hey, why not? So, New Year's Eve, I gave him what he wanted. Aside from the fact that the sex was just godawful, I was trying to start a business, so of course me becoming his exclusive mistress was nowhere in forefront of my mind."

"Using Maritza Wade as your blueprint?" Greg was astonished by not only her choice but by her nerve to confess it.

Jentri scoffed and rolled her eyes. "Yeah, dumb, I know that now. Anyway, I had no plans to stop seeing other clients and one night while out at a cocktail party, I ran into Leland and his wife. He was not too pleased to see me flirting with someone else and kept his distance from me that entire evening. Out the corner of my eye though, I did see him talking to Amelia and her father, they were all staring at me. One week later Leland calls and he's all about the apologies for his behavior and wanting to make it up to me with diamonds and furs and blah, blah, blah. Now, I'm thinking, okay cool, we're back to our old routine. Turns out, we weren't. He had started taping our conversations and cutting the tape at just the right moment to make me sound guilty. He got the idea from Amelia. Apparently, Leland, Amelia, and Amelia's father all had some sort of ax to grind against me and now they've all come together to chop my head off."

Greg stuck his hands back in his pockets and walked back over to the foot of the bed. "So, rather than face up to the consequences of what you did, you're gonna sell out your friend?"

"But I didn't do what they said I did."

"And Ocean didn't do anything at all except maybe trust you." Greg thoughtfully picked at the fuzz balls on the blanket then glanced up at Jentri. "She ran away from home when she was eighteen to get away from her mother, and you, her *friend,* were trying to emulate the one woman she never wanted to become. How is it in good conscience you can sit here and call yourself her *friend* while you're doing that?

There was no excuse for what she'd done, no reasonable explanation. "Mr. Edwards, please, I know what I've done is indefensible, but please, let me fix it—help me and I'll fix it, I promise."

"And how the hell are you going to do that? How do you propose to *fix* it?"

Pulling herself together as best she could, Jentri rolled her shoulders back and wiped the tears from her face. "Amelia's father, that man may love his daughter but he loves me more. After the axes were sharpened, he called me to go meet him for drinks, and he told me what they're planning to do. They're gonna contest the will. Leland is friends with Max's stepmother, they're going to use her to start the petition saying that she's the true *Mrs. Prentiss*, and that Max was manipulated and conned by Ocean, and that he wasn't in his right mind when he married her. That way the money from the estate would be split between you and her. Plus, Amelia would get part of the money plus Max's businesses once she marries you and then she'll have the best portfolio with her firm and since her firm solely deals in corporate law, they'll take on Leland's firm to be the lawyers for the lawyers—that way they all win."

Of all the bad things he'd been through in his life, this truly took the cake. Being deceived by so many people on so many different levels and all at the same time; it was like he had just been punched in the gut. "So, that's what they're planning, is it?"

Jentri nodded, her eyes pleading with Greg to give her a chance. "Please help me fix this and I'll do whatever I have to do to get you the information you need."

Greg turned and headed towards the door. "Stay here with Ocean. I'll be back tomorrow."

CHAPTER THIRTY-EIGHT

In the lower level of the town house that now belonged to him and Ocean, Greg lay in his bed staring up at the ceiling and tried to make sense of his life. In the past it didn't matter when bad things happened or when people treated him like shit. Whatever it was, it didn't matter and whoever may have done it didn't matter; they were insignificant people and events and at the end of the day he was better than fine because he had Max—he *always* had Max. Now, staring at the ceiling, he searched for him, but the hurt it caused trying to see a face that time had stolen from him hurt too much, so he shut his eyes and prayed for numbness. It was in that moment, he understood exactly why Ocean's heart was having such difficulty pumping. Sorrow felt like a ton of bricks laying across his chest and an ice pick shoved into his side; he couldn't breathe and it *hurt*.

As much as he just wanted to stay there and hate life and hate everyone, he promised Max he wouldn't—he wouldn't crawl inside himself, he wouldn't shut down, he'd never stop fighting, never stop living. So he got up, grabbed the bottle of whiskey he'd brought downstairs and he flipped open the door on his entertainment center and searched for the record that played the day he and Max both realized their paths would be inextricably linked. As he pulled the Elvis record from its jacket a letter addressed to him fell out. After putting the record on he sat down on the love seat pressed against the back wall and he slowly fingered the envelope in his hand and tried to prepare his heart for the words from his brother and best friend that lay inside.

Greg-

"You're so fucking predictable, I knew you'd be here. All jokes aside, you must be hurting pretty bad if you're here and you're listening to the one record you refused to listen to since you were thirteen. So, I'll make this quick.

I don't know where I am right now or what I'm doing, but know this brother—I'm missing you. You are not alone in your feelings right now, I am right here with you just as I have always been. I know life for you has been a painful journey and not much about it has always made sense with the exception of the bond that you and I share, but I want you to remember one thing—Life is good. Look beyond all the bullshit and distractions and see life for what it is, which is a gift. And as my parting gift to you, I'm entrusting you with one of life's greatest mysteries—a woman. A woman whose love and loyalty run deeper than any ocean, a woman who will stand by you through every and anything. She is your port in this storm—seek haven with her...I sought her out—for you. I never meant to fall in love with Ocean. I wanted to find someone for you, someone honorable and as worthy of love as you are. I've never met two people more perfect for each other. I want to apologize for falling in love with her,

God knows I tried not to, but I don't regret a second I spent with her.

You and Ocean, you're both so stubborn and so perfectly matched, it brings me joy to know that my child will have a lion and lioness to guard her against the ugliness of the world. You would be wise to let her love you, and it doesn't matter that she loved me first, it only matters that YOU get to love her longer, and I promise you will be a better man for it. I don't expect you to tell her about this letter, in fact, I expect you'll fight the feelings you will inevitably have for her until it drives you crazy. Like I said, you're real fucking predictable. So, put the whiskey down, shake it off and go take care of my girls. I love you and never forget I am ALWAYS with you.

Your brother,
Max

Deciding to have one last squabble with his dearly departed brother, Greg took another swig of whiskey from the bottle. He didn't put the bottle down as instructed but he did change the record to one of his and Max's favorites, Van Morrison *Days Like This*.

***

The following day when he showed up to the hospital Jentri was still there by Ocean's bedside.

"She said anything yet?"

Jentri stretched and looked at Greg somewhat defeated. "Not a word."

At the foot of the hospital bed Greg looked down at Ocean and inhaled deeply. "Okay, Jentri. I'll help you, but I don't want you to *do* anything. Don't see any of them, don't take any of their calls, don't *do* anything. I've got this."

Relief washed over Jentri as if she had just swum up from under a breaker at the beach. "Thank you, thank you, *thank you*. And I won't, I won't make contact with any of them, I swear. Just—*thank you.*"

Greg gave a casual shrug like it was nothing. "You're welcome. You can go now though, I'm gonna sit and talk with Ocean a minute. I'll call you if I need you for anything."

Jentri wanted to rush to Greg and hug him but better judgement prevailed and she quietly left the room.

Just the two of them alone in the room, Greg sat in the seat once occupied by Jentri and studied Ocean's face. "You know they're talking about admitting you to the psych ward. You're not crazy, it would be terrible for you if you let them do that. I know your heart hurts but you've got to..." Greg caught himself before the words came out his mouth. Who was he to tell someone to *move on*? He knew better, he knew there was a certain kind of pain that you couldn't move on from, a type of pain that you just carried with you through life. He knew this pain and he knew there was no *moving on* from it, no out running it and no use trying to hide from it. "Never mind. Anyway, it appears the vultures are circling and they're coming for you. I've decided to fight for you…fight *with* you if you decide to get out of the bed sometime soon, which, I'm hoping you will."

Ocean opened her eyes and looked at Greg. "I know."

"You know? You know, what?" Greg was more confused by her response than the fact that she responded.

"I know you'll fight for me." Ocean's eyes were tired but they weren't hollow anymore. The way she looked at Greg, showed there was still life in her yet.

"And, how exactly did you know that?"

Ocean took a breath that looked like she was trying to pick up the scent of someone's old sweater. "Max told me."

Greg leaned back and studied Ocean's face more intently. "Max told you?"

Ocean smiled. "Max told me. I told him, I didn't think you would, but he told me to trust him, that you were so predictable, that you couldn't help yourself. He said, when it really mattered, when it was worth fighting for,

you'd do the right thing and because you two always
mattered to each other, he said, that I was someone who
would always matter to you also. I thought he was nuts,
but here you are."

Greg exhaled in disbelief. "Max, told you that?"

Ocean closed her eyes and took another whiff of the
invisible sweater. "Max, told me that."

CHAPTER THIRTY-NINE

"We need to make this quick, Gregory, I've got a conference call back at my office at two o'clock." Amelia tapped her Cartier watch as she took her seat around the conference room table at Greg's firm.

Greg took a seat at the head of the table, typically the head of the table was reserved for the senior most partner and everyone else would sit at either side of the table down from where he or she sat, it was a way to show respect...or superiority. Greg sitting at the head of the table for the reading of the will was an exception to the rule, it was a formality, a way to show him respect without actually respecting him. Greg took his seat today feeling neither inferior to anyone at the table or respectful of them. "Now that we're all here, let's begin." Greg folded his hands and leaned forward on the table and looked around.

Feeling somewhat slighted about his position at the table as well as uneasy since he was uncertain about what the meeting topic was on, Leland nosily adjusted himself in his seat and huffed. "Yes, please tell us why we are all here; and why you felt you had to drag Amelia's poor father all the way in to the city."

Amelia looked at her father and smiled as she gently patted the top of his hand. "Oh, Daddy doesn't mind, do you Daddy? He'd do anything for Gregory or me, isn't that right?" Amelia's father looked at her and smiled as he nodded in agreement.

Greg chuckled and rolled his eyes. "Yeah, well, let's get to it, then. This morning, I filed a motion to dismiss. You know, that ridiculous petition you all started? I've filed a motion with the clerk to dismiss it. Your petition contesting Max's will—has no merit. None of you have a leg to stand on." Not having reached the question and answer portion of the meeting Greg waived a dismissive hand at Amelia who was at the edge of her seat ready to interject. "I'm not done. I'm here on behalf of Mrs. Maxwell Prentiss...*the only* living Mrs. Prentiss. As her legal counsel and the executor of her husband's estate, I'm here to let you know that all future actions on behalf of any of you will result in legal action filed by me on her behalf for conspiracy to commit felony theft. Additionally, we will report all of you to the bar association for misconduct."

Distressed and shocked by Greg's statement Amelia was unable to contain herself. "Gregory, I don't know what's come over you. Between Maxwell's death and the whiskey drinking, I'm honestly concerned."

"Don't you pull that shit with me, you conniving, vicious little bitch." Greg's anger and internal temperature was rising, he quickly unbuttoned his suit jacket as he scowled at Amelia.

"Edwards!" Leland slammed his hand down on the table and did his best to stare Greg down and try and take command of the conversation. "Control yourself Edwards. I'll not have you addressing Ms. Walcott in such a manner at my table. She is a lady and you will speak to her with respect.

Greg met Leland's gaze and leaned into it reinforcing his position at the head of the table that day. "*Lady*? That woman is anything but a lady. I had a chat with Jentri and found out what had you so hot and bothered about her and why you were so desperate to land Max as a client. Apparently you're not as talented in the field of blackmail as your father was, which is how he obtained the client list he so graciously gave to you when he retired. If you were, you wouldn't have to *sleep* with your clients to keep those accounts." Greg laughed. "And to think, this whole time you've been looking down your nose at Ocean and where she came from and this whole time you've been doing the same thing. At least Maritza did it to sustain a lifestyle, you're doing it for a portfolio and disguising your indiscretions behind a job you don't even know how to do." Greg barked out a laugh at Amelia and shook his head then turned to back to Leland. "And it's *Prentiss*, you hypocritical pompous blowhard. *Gregory Ian Edwards-Prentiss*."

Amelia laughed and swiveled in her seat. Greg was right about everything he said, she went to work but she didn't actually do much, she was an attorney in name only, she didn't actually litigate anything. The other two men at the table, Leland and her father both knew, they'd always known Amelia had zero talent in the legal field, Greg was the only one who didn't know, which is why she refused to be shaken. She'd been conning Greg for years and she figured she could pull the wool over his eyes one more time. "I know you and Maxwell likened yourselves to brothers but legally you were nothing more than a close friend—more like charity case, and that slutty temp is *not* the only Mrs. Prentiss, in fact she's nothing more than an error in judgment, a side effect of the cancer. Because of her current condition we'll be happy to withdraw our petition as long as she agrees to take what we have to offer—which will be one million dollars and not a penny more and then she walks away. It's a good deal, I strongly urge you to take it."

Clearly, all the pretenses were being dropped, he knew what he said about Amelia was true. He had expected her to at least *try* to convince him it wasn't, or act insulted at least, but no. She heard what he said and she accepted it. Amelia's silent admission was fine with Greg, he hadn't come in there with the intention on spouting pleasantries, he intended to be firm and direct and at the same time as respectful as he could; but now, now the gloves were off. "Go to hell Amelia, you selfish, pretentious piece of garbage. This isn't a corporate merger, not that you would know what that was, let me rephrase… I'm not one of your scumbag clients with my pants down, you're not gonna con or manipulate your way out of this, you're way out of your depth sweetheart. You can't win this." Greg tilted his head and gave Amelia a condescending grin. "Max's estate is worth thirty billion dollars, his liquid assets alone are at sixteen billion and his wife who is so distraught she's been laying in a hospital bed *literally* dying of a broken heart, she whose been so irreparably damaged by the devastation of her husband's death that she's been virtually incapacitated by sorrow—for all she's suffered, for all she's lost—for all her heartache, you want to give her a million dollars? You can go straight to hell, all of you! I hope you all rot in hell. You won't get a cent from Max's estate, any of you." Greg stood up from his seat and scowled at all three blank faces staring back at him. "Furthermore, I've legally borne the name Prentiss since I was thirteen when Max's father adopted me, *legally*. Your scapegoat, the woman pretending to be Max's doting stepmother is going to have a hard time explaining why Mr. Prentiss never bothered to adopt her child when they got married considering how quickly he adopted me. Out of respect for my mother, I've continued to use Edwards to honor the woman who sacrificed everything for me. And yes, she was a woman who had sex with men to keep food on the table but unlike the three of you, my mother was no whore." Greg quickly straightened his jacket and focused his attention on Amelia. "Lastly, you manipulative little bitch, the next time you try and extort someone and use them as a pawn in your little conspiracy, you might want to have a talk with your *dear old dad* and tell him to save the pillow talk for his wife. Also, Amelia, in case you weren't aware and I can see why you might not be considering your vast ignorance of the law. But, bringing up prostitution charges against Ms. McDavid in this case would be an automatic admission of your father's solicitation—and yours Leland, which would be cause for an immediate ethics review." Greg looked at the three of them, he was thoroughly disgusted by the sight of their faces. "You have nothing, you will get nothing, and if any of you pursue this further, I will end all of you." Greg reached into the inside pocket of his jacket and retrieved an envelope which he then tossed at Leland. "My resignation. Effective immediately."

CHAPTER FORTY

One week following Greg's resignation, Ocean was released from the hospital and the two of them were finally peacefully coexisting together in their town house.

In what was shaping up to be a pretty whimsical nursery, Ocean stood over Greg as he put the final pieces of the crib together. "Okay, so I think all that's left is for you to slide that pieces in and then it's done." The difference a week made was amazing, but it wasn't the passing of time that got Ocean out her hospital bed…it was Greg.

"Are you sure? Maybe we should test it with something. What if we put her in and the bottom falls out?" Greg studied the crib he'd very carefully put together and questioned his craftsmanship.

Ocean laughed as she backed away and took a seat in the rocking chair in the corner of the room. "It's fine, Greg." The dusty pink crib fit perfectly with the room's motif. The walls were painted lilac and pink and in lieu of your typical nursery rhyme characters an artist had come in and masterfully recreated some of Degas' best work and covered the walls with tiny little dancers. Also, hanging from the wall right above the crib the original Degas—the reason the room existed in the first place." You worry too much. You're gonna drive yourself crazy always worrying about something bad happening, which reminds me, we have a field trip today."

"A field trip? Where to?" Greg lifted the railing of the crib and leaned inside to push on the mattress and verify that everything was sturdy.

"It's a surprise." After pushing herself out the rocking chair, Ocean smiled and headed for the door. "Give me a head start and I'll meet you by the car in five minutes."

The shared sorrow between the two had made living together surprisingly easy. Their relationship had virtually changed overnight, the one thing—person, that had kept them at odds, was now the thing that had brought them together, there was a shared peace between them. After his final meeting with Amelia, her father and Leland. Greg went back to his condo, packed all of his things, and brought them to the town house. It hardly took any time at all since the town house had always been his real home to begin with, the condo was merely where he shared space with Amelia. A few days after that, he brought Ocean home and they sat up all night listening to Van Morrison, her drinking hot chocolate and him drinking whiskey — the two of them laughing and talking about all the names that Greg had called Amelia and how ironic it was that when it really came down to it, their mothers, Greg's and Ocean's, were more honest and had more integrity than the people who stuck up their noses at them and condemned them. That night Greg and Ocean found their friendship in their common sorrow and shared truth.

One twenty minute ride from downtown Seattle to West Seattle and they had arrived. West Seattle was a little more laid back than the downtown area but it was just as beautiful.

"So, what do you think?" Ocean looked at Greg beaming ear to ear.

In the middle of a vacant lot of an abandoned building, Greg looked around confused. "Think of what?"

Ocean walked towards the entrance of the building. "The area, the building…What do you think? Do you like it?"

Still confused as he followed behind Ocean, Greg searched around trying to figure out why they were there. "Like it for what?"

"For you, silly. Max always said you were so much better than the idiots at the old firm, he always thought you should be in business for yourself. So, anyway I remembered passing this place once when he and I were out and I don't know, I thought maybe it would make a great office for you. So, I bought it. You're too good a lawyer to sit at home all day worrying about me. Plus, I can help out and come and work for you again, help you get things up and running and I promise...I won't give out any legal advice."

Shocked and amused Greg laughed and shook his head trying to rid himself of the astonishment he was feeling. "Your advice wasn't that bad, just not beneficial to business."

"I'll take that as a compliment." Ocean laughed with Greg as she handed him the keys. "And, I was thinking even though I am still kinda pissed off at her, maybe you could hire Jentri—she could be your receptionist or something."

"Ocean this is great but I don't want you wasting all your money on me. Max left it for you."

"What am I going to do with sixteen billion dollars? Besides it'll be fun and the place is big enough you could even have a daycare here and a coffee lounge and...and..." Ocean's brown eyes radiated with excitement and anticipation.

Watching how excited she was got Greg excited too. "*And*, what else?"

"And I think my water broke. That or I—no, I definitely didn't pee myself, that's gross. Yeah, definitely my water broke." Ocean looked down at her legs and frowned.

Panic stricken Greg stared down at her legs too. "No, you've got like four more weeks to go. It's not time yet."

"I think the liquid spreading down my thighs trumps the calendar date." As if the sudden release of fluid was a minor inconvenience, Ocean turned back towards the building and looked back up at Greg. "Don't worry, I think we still have time before anything really starts to happen, you wanna go inside the building and look around?"

"Look inside the building?" Greg put his hands on his hips and looked up at the sky and shook his head. "You're nuts, the both of you—completely nuts, no wonder you got along so well." After giving Max a quick talking to, Greg lowered his head and looked back at Ocean. "You're just as crazy as he was. Always trying to squeeze in just a little more time, stop and smell one more rose." Greg shook his head and smiled. "I don't know about you, but my medical expertise is limited to Tylenol and band aids, so how about we tour the inside another day and head to the hospital?"

It didn't take long for them to reach the hospital back in the downtown area, and while Ocean had some mild discomfort along the ride it wasn't anything she couldn't deal with. The pain was brief and several minutes apart. But all that changed when they walked through the emergency room doors. Almost instantly after being admitted, Ocean's labor kicked into high gear.

"I can't do this. I changed my mind, I don't wanna do this, I wanna go home." Ocean gripped the sides of the bed as the next wave of contractions hit her.

Greg stood back away from the bed nervous about getting too close. "It's a little too late for that." He was nervous but very excited. He couldn't wait to look into the eyes of the little girl making her debut today. He was ready to finally get a glimpse of his friend again.

"You're smiling! Why are you smiling? This isn't funny, I feel like my insides are being ripped out, and you're laughing at me." Ocean tried not to laugh but the sight of Greg's nervous anxious face got the better of her.

"I'm not laughing at you, I swear. I'm just excited to see her—to see what she looks like." Greg rubbed his hands together and glanced at the door. "I'm gonna go grab the nurse and see if they can give you anything for the pain, I'll be right down the hall."

"Down the hall?" Ocean nearly leapt out the bed. "You can't leave!"

Greg raised both his eyebrows in surprise. "Ocean, look, I know we've been getting along great for a while now, but we're not that close yet. I don't need to see that much of you."

Ocean burst into laughter and flinched with pain. "You ass. You can't leave, Greg, you're my family—you're her other dad. You have to stay."

Realizing he was in fact who she said he was, Greg took a step forward closer to the bed. "You know, I meant to ask you about the whole emergency contact thing. I understand Max being on the list, but me? Why not Jentri?"

Slowly releasing air from her cheeks and rubbing her stomach Ocean looked down and smiled the best she could through the pain. "I have never been sick, being pregnant is really the only time I've ever had to visit a hospital other than a yearly checkup, so I wasn't really thinking about me when I choose you, I was thinking about her. If something ever happened to me, who would I trust with my child's life. As big of an ass as you can be, I know besides me and Max, there's no one in the world who would ever love her like you will. It wasn't a hard choice to make."

After three hours of labor that afternoon, Mercy Grace Prentiss made her arrival into the world. She was four weeks early but healthy and happy none the less.

After a few hours of sleep, Ocean woke up that evening to see Greg slowly pacing the floor with Mercy in his arms. "Why do they always have to die?" As she looked at the little pink cap poking out the blanket Ocean's eyes welled up with tears.

Slowly making his way to her bedside Greg sighed as he looked down at Mercy's face. "He didn't—look at her—Maxwell Prentiss is alive and well in this little girl. He wasn't dying when he was with you either, I'm sorry I said that to you before. He wasn't dying. He was living; and in all the years that I've known him I've never seen him more alive then when he was spending his final days with you."

As Greg sat down on the side of the bed, Ocean reached out and touched the little pink cap and smiled. "You know, he used to try and help me think of ways to win you over." Ocean chuckled as she thought back over their tumultuous past. "I don't think I've ever tried harder in my life to get someone to like me but I knew if it came down to it and he had to choose... he'd always choose you. I get it, though, and I admired him so much for that. I was also jealous as hell. I never had anyone in my life that loved me the way you two loved each other. You guys had a bond, a loyalty to one another and it was truly humbling to see; it was more beautiful than any piece of artwork in existence."

"Yeah, well, I know all the dark and twisted secrets he had in his heart and he knew the perilousness of mine. He really was my soul brother." Greg passed Mercy to Ocean and gently brushed her cheek with his finger.

"You didn't have to work as hard as you did by the way. I didn't hate you. I never hated you."

***

After a brief hospital stay, Ocean, Greg and Mercy returned back to the townhome. While she was still in the maternity ward she was never alone, if it wasn't Greg at her side it was Jentri. She and Ocean managed to mend fences over the course of her visits and get back to laughing with one another again.

Ocean and Greg had been back at the town house with the baby almost a full week and they pretty much had a routine developed for taking care of Mercy. Neither Ocean or Greg thought they'd be good parents and neither had spent any time with children, but for two novices they were doing a pretty good job. Ocean was a night owl so that was her shift, and Greg was an early riser so that was his; but neither was ever too tired to take care of the baby and they were both equally obsessed with the tiny little girl.

At six o'clock Saturday evening their parental jitters were starting to show through. Maybe it's the storm." Ocean looked out the window desperately trying to will Mother Nature to calm the skies. The skies outside were dark and the inside of the town home was as well, they had managed to find some candles and give the main areas they occupied a soft glow.

Greg bounced Mercy in his arms as he walked around the living room. "She's not hungry and I just changed her…I don't know. You think she's sick? She's never cried this much before."

Ocean didn't know what it was but she wanted it to stop. The sound of her baby girl crying was nearly bringing her to tears. Then like lightening, it hit her, her own desire to cry suddenly struck a chord with her. "Sympathy pains."

Confused Greg turned around and frowned. "What?"

Ocean laughed. "Sympathy pains." Ocean looked at Greg waiting for him to nod in understanding, but then she realized how unreasonable and confusing she was being in that moment. "When Max and I were on our honeymoon my morning sickness was really bad and I was always needing a nap and throwing up and Max— mind you I didn't know he was sick at the time, Max was always throwing up and sleeping all the time too. He said it must have been sympathy pains. He told me he read all about it on google or whatever, but anyway back to my point. We'd nap together and he'd rub my stomach and hum until I fell asleep."

Greg was still confused. "What does that have to do with Mercy crying?"

Ocean moved from the window and began heading down the hall. "Follow me. I have an idea." In the candle lit darkness of the library Ocean ushered Greg to the couch. "Lay down and let her rest on your chest, she's upset because we're upset. So, instead of focusing on her—I'm gonna focus on you."

Not understanding but doing as he was instructed, Greg laid down and laid Mercy on his chest. No sooner had he laid down did he hear the chord of a piano key which was quickly followed by Ocean singing. She hadn't sung more than three lines and already Mercy was calming down. Greg looked down at Mercy and sighed with relief, then over at Ocean who was smiling at him, her big brown eyes and thick curly locks were accentuated by the candlelight; the entire scene was completely mesmerizing.

The clarity of the piano chords, Ocean's somber yet soulful voice and one of his favorite songs. He'd listened to Elvis all his life but listening to Ocean sing was like hearing the song for the first time. He was completely captivated. The lyrics to *Can't Help Falling in Love* never made more sense to him then it did in that moment. He silently cursed Max and his predictions and while he wasn't in love with Ocean in that moment, he decided not to try and fight fate just to prove a ghost wrong. He never won an argument with Max while he was alive, it gave Greg a sense of comfort to know that even in death he still couldn't win; he smiled at the realization that death, while it had taken Max from him it didn't take that, it couldn't take everything. In fact, it had given him more then he could have ever hoped for.

CPSIA information can be obtained
at www.ICGtesting.com
Printed in the USA
LVHW090603160321
681656LV00013B/307